KU-317-607

HIS CINDERELLA HEIRESS

BY

MARION LENNOX

ST HELENS
COMMUNITY
LIBRARIES

ACC. №

F16

CLASS №

MILLS &
BOON

All rights reserved including the right of reproduction
in whole or in part in any form. This edition is published
by arrangement with Harlequin Books S.A.

This is a work of fiction. Names, characters, places,
locations and incidents are purely fictional and bear
no relationship to any real life individuals, living or
dead, or to any actual places, business establishments,
locations, events or incidents. Any resemblance is entirely
coincidental.

This book is sold subject to the condition that it shall not,
by way of trade or otherwise, be lent, resold, hired out
or otherwise circulated without the prior consent of the
publisher in any form of binding or cover other than that
in which it is published and without a similar condition
including this condition being imposed on the subsequent
purchaser.

® and TM are trademarks owned and used by the
trademark owner and/or its licensee. Trademarks
marked with ® are registered with the United Kingdom
Patent Office and/or the Office for Harmonisation in the
Internal Market and in other countries.

First published in Great Britain 2016
By Mills & Boon, an imprint of HarperCollins*Publishers*
1 London Bridge Street, London, SE1 9GF

Large Print edition 2016

© 2016 Marion Lennox

ISBN: 978-0-263-26258-2

Our policy is to use papers that are natural, renewable
and recyclable products and made from wood grown
in sustainable forests. The logging and manufacturing
processes conform to the legal environmental regulations
of the country of origin.

Printed and bound in Great Britain
by CPI Antony Rowe, Chippenham, Wiltshire

HIS CINDERELLA
HEIRESS

To Mitzi. My shadow.

CHAPTER ONE

A WOMAN WAS stuck in his bog.

Actually, Finn Conaill wasn't sure if this land was part of the estate, but even if this wasn't the property of the new Lord of Glenconaill he could hardly ignore a woman stuck in mud to her thighs.

He pulled off the road, making sure the ground he steered onto was solid.

A motorbike was parked nearby and he assumed it belonged to the woman who was stuck. To the unwary, the bike was on ground that looked like a solid grass verge. She'd been lucky. The wheels had only sunk a couple of inches.

She'd not been so lucky herself. She was a hundred yards from the road, and she looked stuck fast.

'Stay still,' he called.

'Struggling makes me sink deeper.' Her voice sounded wobbly and tired.

'Then don't struggle.'

Of all the idiot tourists... She could have been here all night, he thought, as he picked his way carefully across to her. This road was a little used shortcut across one of County Galway's vast bogs. The land was a sweep of sodden grasses, dotted with steel-coloured washes of ice-cold water. In the distance he could see the faint outline of Castle Glenconaill, its vast stone walls seemingly merging into the mountains behind it. There'd been a few tough sheep on the road from the village, but here there was nothing.

There was therefore no one but Finn to help.

'Can you come faster?' she called and he could hear panic.

'Only if you want us both stuck. You're in no danger. I'm coming as fast as I can.'

Though he wouldn't mind coming faster. He'd told the housekeeper at the castle he'd arrive mid-afternoon and he was late already.

He spent considerable time away from his farm now, researching farming methods, investigating innovative ideas, so he had the staff to take care of the day-to-day farming. He'd been prepared to leave early this morning, with his manager more than ready to take over.

But then Maeve had arrived from Dublin, glamorous, in designer clothes and a low-slung sports car. She looked a million light years away from the woman who'd torn around the farm with him as a kid—who once upon a time he was sure he wanted to spend his life with. After a year apart—she'd asked for twelve months 'to discover myself before we marry'—what she'd told him this morning had only confirmed what he already knew. Their relationship was over, but she'd been in tears and he owed her enough to listen.

And then, on top of everything else, there'd been trouble lambing. He'd bottle-fed Sadie from birth, she was an integral part of a tiny flock of sheep he was starting to build, and he hadn't had the heart to leave until she was safely delivered.

Finally he'd tugged on clean trousers, a decent shirt and serviceable boots, and there was an end to his preparation for inheriting title and castle. If the castle didn't approve, he'd decided, it could find itself another lord.

And now he was about to get muddy, which wasn't very lordly either.

At least he knew enough of bogland to move slowly, and not get into trouble himself. He knew innocuous grassland often overlaid mud and running water. It could give way at any moment. The only way to tread safely was to look for rocks that were big enough to have withstood centuries of sodden land sucking them down.

After that initial panicked call, the woman was now silent and still, watching him come. The ground around her was a mire, churned. The bog wasn't so dangerous that it'd suck her down like quicksand, but it was thick and claggy so, once she'd sunk past her knees, to take one step after another back to dry land would have proved impossible.

He was concentrating on his feet and she was concentrating on watching him. Which he appreciated. He had no intention of ending up stuck too.

When he was six feet away he stopped. From here the ground was a churned mess. A man needed to think before going further.

'Thank you for coming,' she said.

He nodded, still assessing.

She sounded Australian, he thought, and she was young, or youngish, maybe in her mid to late twenties. Her body was lithe, neat and trim. She had short cropped, burnt-red curls. Wide green eyes were framed by long dark lashes. Her face was spattered with freckles and smeared with mud; eyeliner and mascara were smudged down her face. She had a couple of piercings in one ear and four in the other.

She was wearing full biker gear, black, black and black, and she was gazing up at him almost defiantly. Her thanks had seemed forced—like *I know I've been stupid but I defy you to tell me I am.*

His lips twitched a little. He could tell her anything he liked—she was in no position to argue.

'You decided to take a stroll?' he asked, taking time to assess the ground around her.

'I read about this place on the Internet.' Still he could hear the defiance. Plus the accent. With those drawn-out vowels, she had to be Australian. 'It said this district was famous for its quaking bogs but they weren't dangerous. I asked in the village and the guy I asked said the same. He said if you found a soft part, you could jump up and down and it bounced. So I did.'

His brows lifted. 'Until it gave way?'

'The Internet didn't say anything about sinking. Neither did the guy I asked.'

'I'd imagine whoever you asked assumed you'd be with someone. This place is safe enough if you're with a friend who can tug you out before you get stuck.'

'I was on my bike. He knew I was alone.'

'Then he'd be trying to be helpful.' Finn was looking at the churned-up mud around her, figuring how stuck she truly was. 'He wouldn't be wanting to disappoint you. Folk around here are like that.'

'Very helpful!' She glowered some more. 'Stupid bog.'

'It's a bit hard to sue a bog, though,' he said gently. 'Meanwhile, I'll fetch planks from the truck. There's no way I'll get you out otherwise. I've no wish to be joining you.'

'Thank you,' she said again, and once more it was as if the words were forced out of her. She was independent, he thought. And feisty. He could see anger and frustration—and also fury that she was dependent on his help.

She was also cold. He could hear it in the quaver in her voice, and by the shudders and chattering teeth she was trying to disguise. Cold and scared? But she wasn't letting on.

'Hold on then,' he said. 'I'll not be long. Don't go anywhere.'

She clamped her lips tight and he just knew the effort it was taking her not to swear.

To say Jo Conaill was feeling stupid would be an understatement. Jo—Josephine on her birth certificate but nowhere else—was feeling as if the ground had been pulled from under her. Which maybe it had.

Of all the dumb things to do...

She'd landed in Dublin two nights ago, spent twenty-four hours fighting off jet lag after the flight from Sydney, then hired a bike and set off.

It was the first time she'd ever been out of Australia and she was in Ireland. Ireland! She didn't feel the least bit Irish, but her surname was Irish and every time she looked in the mirror she felt Irish. Her name and her looks were her only connection to this place, but then, Jo had very few connections to anything. Or anyone.

She was kind of excited to be here.

She'd read about this place before she came—of course she had. Ireland's bogs were legion. They were massive, mysterious graveyards of ancient forests, holding treasures from thousands of years ago. On the Internet they'd seemed rain-swept, misty and beautiful.

On her lunch break, working as a waitress in a busy café on Sydney Harbour, she'd watched a You Tube clip of a couple walking across a bog just like this. They'd been jumping up and down, making each other bounce on the spongy surface.

Jumping on the bogs of Galway. She'd thought maybe she could.

And here she was. The map had shown her this road, describing the country as a magnificent example of undisturbed bog. The weather had been perfect. The bog looked amazing, stretching almost to the horizon on either side of her bike. Spongy. Bouncy. And she wasn't stupid. She had stopped to ask a local and she'd been reassured.

So she'd jumped, just a little at first and then venturing further from the road to get a better bounce. And then the surface had given way and she'd sunk to her knees. She'd struggled for half an hour until she was stuck to her thighs. Then she'd resigned herself to sit like a dummy and wait for rescue.

So here she was, totally dependent on a guy

who had the temerity to laugh. Okay, he hadn't
laughed out loud but she'd seen his lips twitch.
She knew a laugh when she saw one.

At least he seemed...solid. Built for rescuing
women from bogs? He was large, six-two or -three,
muscular, lean and tanned, with a strongly boned
face. He was wearing moleskin trousers and a
khaki shirt, open-necked, his sleeves rolled above
the elbows to reveal brawny arms.

He was actually, decidedly gorgeous, she conceded. Definitely eye candy. In a different situation she might even have paused to enjoy. He had
the weathered face and arms of a farmer. His hair
was a deep brown with just a hint of copper—
a nod to the same Irish heritage she had? It was
wavy but cropped short and serviceable. His deep
green eyes had crease lines at the edges—from
exposure to weather?

Or from laughter.

Probably from laughter, she decided. His eyes
were laughing now.

Eye candy or not, she was practically gritting
her chattering teeth as she waited for him. She was
totally dependent on a stranger. She, Jo Conaill,
who was dependent on nobody.

He was heading back, carrying a couple of short planks, moving faster now he'd assessed the ground. His boots were heavy and serviceable. Stained from years of work on the land?

'I have a bull who keeps getting himself bogged near the water troughs,' he said idly, almost as if he was talking to himself and not her. 'If these planks can get Horace out, they'll work for you. That is if you don't weigh more than a couple of hundred pounds.'

Laughter was making his green eyes glint. His smile, though, was kind.

She didn't want kind. She wanted to be out of here.

'Don't try and move until they're in place,' he told her. 'Horace always messes that up. First sign of the planks and he's all for digging himself in deeper.'

'You're comparing me to a bull?'

He'd stooped to set the planks in place. Now he sat back on his heels and looked at her. Really looked. His gaze raked her, from the top of her dishevelled head to where her leather-clad legs disappeared into the mud.

The twinkle deepened.

'No,' he said at last. 'No, indeed. I'll not compare you to a bull.'

And he chuckled.

If she could, she'd have closed her eyes and drummed her heels. Instead, she had to manage a weak smile. She had to wait. She was totally in this man's hands and she didn't like it one bit.

It was her own fault. She'd put herself in a position of dependence and she depended on nobody.

Except this man.

'So what do they call you?' He was manoeuvring the planks, checking the ground under them, setting them up so each had a small amount of rock underneath to make them secure. He was working as if he had all the time in the world. As if she did.

She didn't. She was late.

She was late and covered in bog.

'What would who call me?' she snapped.

'Your Mam and Daddy?'

As if. 'Jo,' she said through gritted teeth.

'Just Jo?'

'Just Jo.' She glared.

'Then I'm Finn,' he said, ignoring her glare. 'I'm pleased to meet you, Just Jo.' He straightened, putting his weight on the planks, seeing how far they sank. He was acting as if he pulled people out of bogs all the time.

No. He pulled bulls out of bogs, she thought, and that was what she felt like. A stupid, bog-stuck bovine.

'You're Australian?'

'Yes,' she said through gritted teeth, and he nodded as if Australians stuck in bogs were something he might have expected.

'Just admiring the view, were we?' The laughter was still in his voice, an undercurrent to his rich Irish brogue, and it was a huge effort to stop her teeth from grinding in frustration. Except they were too busy chattering.

'I'm admiring the frogs,' she managed. 'There are frogs in here. All sorts.'

He smiled, still testing the planks, but his smile said he approved of her attempt to join him in humour.

'Fond of frogs?'

'I've counted eight since I've been stuck.'

He grinned. 'I'm thinking that's better than counting sheep. If you'd nodded off I might not have seen you from the road.' He stood back, surveyed her, surveyed his planks and then put a boot on each end of the first plank and started walking. The end of the planks were a foot from her. He went about two-thirds along, then stopped and crouched. And held out his hands.

'Right,' he said. 'Put your hands in mine. Hold fast. Then don't struggle, just let yourself relax and let me pull.'

'I can...'

'You can't do anything,' he told her. 'If you struggle you'll make things harder. You can wiggle your toes if you like; that'll help with the suction, but don't try and pull out. If you were Horace I'd be putting a chain under you but Horace isn't good at following orders. If you stay limp like a good girl, we'll have you out of here in no time.'

Like a good girl. The patronising toerag...

He was saving her. What was she doing resenting it? Anger was totally inappropriate. But then, she had been stuck for almost an hour, growing more and more furious with herself. She'd also been more than a little bit frightened by the time he'd arrived. And cold. Reaction was setting in and she was fighting really hard to hold her temper in check.

'Where's a good wall to kick when you need it?' Finn asked and she blinked.

'Pardon?'

'I'd be furious too, if I were you. The worst thing in the world is to want to kick and all you have to kick is yourself.'

She blinked. Laughter and empathy too? 'S... sorry.'

'That's okay. Horace gets tetchy when he gets stuck, so I'd imagine you're the same. Hands— put 'em in mine and hold.'

'They're covered in mud. You won't be able to hold me.'

'Try me,' he said and held out his hands and waited for her to put hers in his.

It felt wrong. To hold this guy's hands and let her pull...Jo Conaill spent her life avoiding dependence on anyone or anything.

What choice did she have? She put out her hands and held.

His hands were broad and toughened from manual work. She'd guessed he was a farmer, and his hands said she was right. He manoeuvred his fingers to gain maximum hold and she could feel the strength of him. But he was wincing.

'You're icy. How long have you been here?'

'About an hour.'

'Is that right?' He was shifting his grip, trying for maximum hold. 'Am I the first to come along? Is this road so deserted, then?'

'You're not a local?'

'I'm not.' He was starting to take her weight, sitting back on his heels and leaning backward. Edging back as the planks started to tilt.

The temptation to struggle was almost irresistible but she knew it wouldn't help. She forced herself to stay limp.

Channel Horace, she told herself.

'Good girl,' Finn said approvingly and she thought: *What—did the guy have the capacity to read minds?*

He wasn't pulling hard. He was simply letting his weight tug her forward, shifting only to ease the balance of the planks. But his hold was implacable, a steady, relentless pull, and finally she felt the squelch as the mud eased its grip. She felt her feet start to lift. At last.

He still wasn't moving fast. His tug was slow and steady, an inch at a time. He was acting as if he had all the time in the world.

'So I'm not a local,' he said idly, as if they were engaged in casual chat, not part of a chain where half the chain was stuck in mud. 'But I'm closer to home than you are.'

He manoeuvred himself back a little without lessening his grip. He was trying not to lurch back, she realised. If he pulled hard, they both risked being sprawled off the planks, with every chance of being stuck again.

He had had experience in this. With Horace.

'Horace is heavier than you,' he said.

'Thanks. Did you say…two hundred pounds?'

'I did, and I'm thinking you're not a sliver over a hundred and ninety. That's with mud attached,' he added kindly. 'What part of Australia do you come from?'

'S…Sydney.' Sometimes.

'I've seen pictures.' Once more he stopped and readjusted. 'Nice Opera House.'

'Yeah.' It was hard to get her voice to work. He'd released her hands so he could shift forward and hold her under her arms. Once more he was squatting and tugging but now she was closer to him. Much closer. She could feel the strength of him, the size. She could feel the warmth of his chest against her face. The feeling was…weird. She wanted to sink against him. She wanted to struggle.

Sinking won.

'We…we have great beaches too,' she managed and was inordinately proud of herself for getting the words out.

'What, no mud?'

'No mud.'

'Excellent. Okay, sweetheart, we're nearly there. Just relax and let me do the work.'

He had her firmly under the arms and he was leaning back as she forced herself to relax against him. To let him hold her…

The feeling was indescribable—and it worked!

For finally the mud released its grip. Even then, though, he was still in control. He had her tight, hauling her up and back so that she was kneeling on the planks with him, but she wasn't released. He was holding her hard against him, and for a moment she had no choice but to stay exactly where she was.

She'd been stuck in mud for an hour. She was bone-chillingly cold, and she'd been badly frightened. Almost as soon as the mud released her she started to shake.

If he didn't hold her she could have fallen right off the planks. No, she *would* have fallen. She felt light-headed and a bit sick.

He held and she had to let him hold. She needed him.

Which was crazy. She didn't need anyone. She'd made that vow as a ten-year-old, in the fourth or fifth of her endless succession of foster homes. She'd yelled it as her foster mother had tried to explain why she had to move on yet again.

'It's okay,' she'd yelled. 'I don't need you. I don't need anyone.'

Her foster mother had cried but Jo hadn't. She'd learned to never let herself close enough to cry.

But now she was close, whether she willed it or not. Her rescuer was holding her in a grip so strong she couldn't break it even if she tried. He must be feeling her shaking, she thought, and part of her was despising herself for being weak but most of her was just letting him hold.

He was big and warm and solid, and he wasn't letting her go. Her face was hard against his chest. She could feel the beating of his heart.

His hand was stroking her head, as he'd stroke an injured animal. 'Hey there. You're safe. The nasty bog's let you go. A nice hot bath and you'll be right back to yourself again. You're safe, girl. Safe.'

She hadn't been unsafe, she thought almost hysterically, and then she thought maybe she had been. If he hadn't come... Hypothermia was a killer. She could have become one of those bog bodies she'd read about, found immaculately preserved from a thousand years ago. They'd have put her in a museum and marvelled at her beloved bike leathers...

'There was never a chance of it,' Finn murmured into her hair and his words shocked her into reaction.

'What?'

'Freezing to your death out here. There's sheep wandering these bogs. I'm thinking a farmer'll come out and check them morn and night. If I hadn't come along, he would have.'

'But if you're not...if you're not local, how do you know?' she demanded.

'Because the sheep I passed a way back look well cared for, and you don't get healthy sheep without a decent shepherd. You were never in real danger.' He released her a little, but his hands still held her shoulders in case she swayed. 'Do you think you can make it back to the road?'

And then he frowned, looking down at her. 'You're still shaking. We don't want you falling into the mud again. Well, this is something I wouldn't be doing with Horace.'

And, before she could even suspect what he intended, he'd straightened, reached down and lifted her into his arms, then turned towards the road.

She froze.

She was close to actually freezing. From her thighs down, she was soaking. She'd been hauled up out of the mud, into this man's arms, and he was carrying her across the bog as if she weighed little more than a sack of flour.

She was powerless, and the lifelong sense of panic rose and threatened to drown her.

She wanted to scream, to kick, to make him dump her, even if it meant she sank into the bog again. She couldn't do anything. She just…froze.

But then, well before they reached the road, he was setting her down carefully on a patch of bare rock so there was no chance she'd pitch into the mud. But he didn't let her go. He put his hands on her shoulders and twisted her to face him.

'Problem?'

'I...no.'

'You were forgetting to breathe,' he said, quite gently. 'Breathing's important. I'm not a medical man, but I'd say breathing's even more important than reaching solid ground.'

Had her intake of breath been so dramatic that he'd heard it—that he'd felt it? She felt ashamed and silly, and more than a little small.

'You're safe,' he repeated, still with that same gentleness. 'I'm a farmer. I've just finished helping a ewe with a difficult lambing. Helping creatures is what I do for a living. I won't hurt you. I'll clean the muck off you as best I can, then put your bike in the back of my truck and drive you to wherever you can get yourself a hot shower and a warm bed for the night.'

And that was enough to make her pull herself together. She'd been a wimp, an idiot, an absolute dope, and here she was, making things worse. This man was a Good Samaritan. Yeah, well, she'd had plenty of them in her life, but that didn't mean she shouldn't be grateful. He didn't need her stupid baggage and he was helping her. Plus he was gorgeous. That shouldn't make a difference but she'd be an idiot not to be aware of it. She made a massive effort, took a few deep breaths and tugged her dignity around her like a shield.

'Thank you,' she managed, tilting her face until she met his gaze full-on. Maybe that was a mistake. Green eyes met green eyes and something flickered in the pit of her stomach. He was looking at her with compassion but also...something else? There were all sorts of emotions flickering behind those eyes of his. Yes, compassion, and also laughter, but also...empathy? Understanding?

As if he understood what had caused her to fear.

Whatever, she didn't like it. He might be gorgeous. He might have saved her, but she needed to be out of here.

'I can take care of myself from here,' she managed. 'If you just walk across to the road, I'll follow in your footsteps.'

'Take my hand,' he said, still with that strange tinge of understanding that was deeply unsettling. 'You're shaky and if you fall that's time wasted for both of us.'

It was reasonable. It even made sense but only

she knew how hard it was to place her hand in his and let him lead her back to the road. But he didn't look at her again. He watched the ground, took careful steps then turned and watched her feet, making sure her feet did exactly the same.

Her feet felt numb, but the leathers and biker boots had insulated her a little. She'd be back to normal in no time, she thought, and finally they stepped onto the glorious solid road and she felt like bending down and kissing it.

Stupid bogs. The Irish could keep them.

Wasn't she Irish? Maybe she'd disinherit that part of her.

'Where can I take you?' Finn was saying and she stared down at her legs, at the thick, oozing mud, and then she looked at her bike and she made a decision.

'Nowhere. I'm fine.' She forced herself to look up at him, meeting his gaze straight on. 'Honest. I'm wet and I'm dirty but I don't have far to go. This mud will come off in a trice.'

'You're too shaken to ride.'

'I *was* too shaken to ride,' she admitted. 'But now I'm free I'm not shaking at all.' And it was true. Jo Conaill was back in charge of herself again and she wasn't about to let go. 'Thank you so much for coming to my rescue. I'm sorry I've made you muddy too.'

'Not very muddy,' he said and smiled, a lazy, crooked smile that she didn't quite get. It made her feel a bit...melting. Out of control again? She didn't like it.

And then she noticed his feet. His boots were still clean. Clean! He'd hauled her out of the bog and, apart from a few smears of mud where he'd held her, and the fact that his hands were muddy, he didn't have a stain on him.

'How did you do that?' she breathed and his smile intensified. 'How did you stay almost clean?'

'I told you. I'm an old hand at pulling creatures out of trouble. Now, if you were a lamb I'd take you home, rub you down and put you by the fire-stove for a few hours. Are you sure I can't do that for you?'

And suddenly, crazily, she wanted to say yes. She was still freezing. She was still shaking inside. She could have this man take her wherever he was going and put her by his fireside. Part of her wanted just that.

Um...not. She was Jo Conaill and she didn't accept help. Well, okay, sometimes she had to, like when she was dumb enough to try jumping on bogs, but enough. She'd passed a village a few miles back. She could head back there, beg a wash at the pub and then keep on going.

As she always kept going.

'Thank you, no,' she managed and bent and wiped her mud-smeared hands on the grass. Then she finished the job by drying them on the inside of her jacket. She gave him a determined nod, then snagged her helmet from the back of her bike. She shoved it onto her head, clicked the strap closed—only she knew what an effort it was to make her numb fingers work—and then hauled the handles of her bike around.

The bike was heavy. The shakiness of her legs wouldn't quite support...

But there he was, putting her firmly aside, hauling her bike around so it was facing the village. 'That's what you want?'

'I...yes.'

'You're really not going far?'

'N... No. Just to the village.'

'Are you sure you'll be fine?'

'I'm sure,' she managed and hit the ignition and her bike roared into unsociable life. 'Thank you,' she said again over its roar. 'If I can ever do anything for you...'

'Where will I find you?' he asked and she tried a grin.

'On the road,' she said. 'Look for Jo.'

And she gave him a wave with all the insouciance she could muster and roared off into the distance.

CHAPTER TWO

As CASTLES WENT, it seemed a very grand castle. But then, Finn hadn't seen the inside of many castles.

Mrs O'Reilly, a little, round woman with tired eyes and capable, worn hands, bustled into the dining room and placed his dinner before him. It was a grand dinner too, roast beef with vegetables and a rich gravy, redolent of red wine and fried onions. It was a dinner almost fit for…a lord?

'There you are, My Lord,' the housekeeper said and beamed as she stood back and surveyed her handiwork. 'Eh, but it's grand to have you here at last.'

But Finn wasn't feeling grand. He was feeling weird.

My Lord. It was his title. He'd get rid of it, he decided. Once the castle was sold he didn't need to use it. He wasn't sure if he could ever officially abandon it but the knowledge of its existence could stay in the attic at the farm, along with other family relics. Maybe his great-great-great-grandson would like to use it. That was, if there ever was a great-great-great-grandson.

He thought suddenly of Maeve. Would she have liked to be My Lady? Who knew? He was starting to accept that he'd never known Maeve at all. Loyalty, habit, affection—he'd thought they were the basis for a marriage. But over the last twelve months, as he'd thrown himself into improving the farm, looking at new horizons himself, he'd realised it was no basis at all.

But Maeve's father would have liked this, he thought, staring around the great, grand dining room with a carefully neutral expression. He didn't want to hurt the housekeeper's feelings, but dining alone at a table that could fit twenty, on fine china, with silver that spoke of centuries of use, the family crest emblazoned on every piece, with a vast silver epergne holding pride of place in the centre of the shining mahogany of the table... Well, it wasn't exactly his style.

He had a good wooden table back at his farm. It was big enough for a man to have his computer and bookwork at one end and his dinner at the other. A man didn't need a desk with that kind of table, and he liked it that way.

But this was his heritage. His. He gazed out at the sheep grazing in the distance, at the land stretching to the mountains beyond, and he felt a stir of something within that was almost primeval.

This was Irish land, a part of his family. His side of the family had been considered of no import for generations but still...some part of him felt a tug that was almost like the sensation of coming home. Finn was one of six brothers. His five siblings had left their impoverished farm as soon as they could manage. They were now scattered across the globe but, apart from trips to the States to check livestock lines, or attending conferences to investigate the latest in farming techniques, Finn had never wanted to leave. Over the years he'd built the small family plot into something he could be proud of.

But now, this place...why did it feel as if it was part of him?

There was a crazy thought.

'Is everything as you wish?' Mrs O'Reilly asked anxiously.

He looked at her worried face and he gazed

around and thought how much work must have gone into keeping this room perfect. How could one woman do it?

'It's grand,' he told her, and took a mouthful of the truly excellent beef. 'Wonderful.'

'I'm pleased. If there's anything else...'

'There isn't.'

'I don't know where the woman is. The lawyer said mid-afternoon...'

He still wasn't quite sure who the woman was. Details from the lawyers had been sparse, to say the least. 'The lawyer said you'd be expecting me mid-afternoon too,' he said mildly, attacking a bit more of his beef. Yeah, the epergne was off-putting—were they tigers?—but this was excellent food. 'Things happen.'

'Well,' the woman said with sudden asperity, 'she's Fiona's child. We could expect anything.'

'You realise I don't know anything about her. I don't even know who Fiona is,' he told her and the housekeeper narrowed her eyes, as if asking, *How could he not know?* Her look said the whole world should know, and be shocked as well.

'Fiona was Lord Conaill's only child,' she said tersely. 'His Lady died in childbirth. Fiona was a daughter when he wanted a son, but he gave her whatever she wanted. This would have been a cold place for a child and you can forgive a lot through upbringing, but Fiona had her chances and she never took them. She ran with a wild lot and there was nothing she wanted more than to shock her father. And us... The way she treated the servants... Dirt, we were. She ran through her father's money like it was water, entertaining her no-good friends, having parties, making this place a mess, but His Lordship would disappear to his club in Dublin rather than stop her. She was a spoiled child and then a selfish woman. There were one too many parties, though. She died of a drug overdose ten years ago, with only His Lordship to mourn her passing.'

'And her child?'

'Lord Conaill would hardly talk of her,' she said primly. 'For his daughter to have a child out of wedlock... Eh, it must have hurt. Fiona threw it in his face over and over, but still he kept silent. But then he wouldn't talk about you either and you were his heir. Is there anything else you'll be needing?'

'No, thank you,' Finn said. 'Are you not eating?'

'In the kitchen, My Lord,' she said primly. 'It's not my place to be eating here. I'll be keeping another dinner hot for the woman, just in case, but if she's like her mother we may never hear.'

And she left him to his roast beef.

For a while the meal took his attention—a man who normally cooked for himself was never one to be ignoring good food—but when it was finished he was left staring down the shining surface of the ostentatious table, at the pouncing tigers on the epergne, at his future.

What to do with this place?

Sell it? Why not?

The inheritance had come out of the blue. Selling it would mean he could buy the farms bordering his, and the country down south was richer than here. He was already successful but the input of this amount of money could make him one of the biggest primary producers in Ireland.

The prospect should make him feel on top of the world. Instead, he sat at the great, grand dining table and felt...empty. Weird.

He thought of Maeve and he wondered if this amount of money would have made a difference.

It wouldn't. He knew it now. His life had been

one of loyalty—eldest son of impoverished farmers, loyal to his parents, to his siblings, to his farm. And to Maeve.

He'd spent twelve months realising loyalty was no basis for marriage.

He thought suddenly of the woman he'd pulled out of the bog. He hoped she'd be safe and dry by now. He had a sudden vision of her, bathed and warmed, ensconced in a cosy pub by a fire, maybe with a decent pie and a pint of Guinness.

He'd like to be there, he thought. Inheritance or not, right now maybe he'd rather be with her than in a castle.

Or not. What he'd inherited was a massive responsibility. It required...more loyalty?

And loyalty was his principle skill, he thought ruefully. It was what he accepted, what he was good at, and this inheritance was enough to take a man's breath away. Meanwhile the least he could do was tackle more of Mrs O'Reilly's excellent roast beef, he decided, and he did.

If she had anywhere else to go, she wouldn't be here. *Here* scared her half to death.

Jo was cleaned up—sort of—but she was still wet and she was still cold.

She was sitting on her bike outside the long driveway to Castle Glenconaill.

The castle was beautiful.

But this was no glistening white fairy tale, complete with turrets and spires, with pennants and heraldic banners fluttering in the wind. Instead, it seemed carved from the very land it was built on—grey-white stone, rising to maybe three storeys, but so gradually it gave the impression of a vast, long, low line of battlements emerging from the land. The castle was surrounded by farmland, but the now empty moat and the impressive battlements and the mountains looming behind said this castle was built to repel any invader.

As it was repelling her. It was vast and wonderful. It was…scary.

But she was cold. And wet. A group of stone cottages were clustered around the castle's main gates but they all looked derelict, and it was miles back to the village. And she'd travelled half a world because she'd just inherited half of what lay before her.

'This is my ancestral home,' she muttered and shivered and thought, *Who'd want a home like this?*

Who'd want a home? She wanted to turn and run.

But she was cold and she was getting colder. The wind was biting. She'd be cold even if her leathers weren't wet, she thought, but her leathers were wet and there was nowhere to stay in the village and, dammit, she had just inherited half this pile.

'But if they don't have a bath I'm leaving,' she muttered.

Where would she go?

She didn't know and she didn't care. There was always somewhere. But the castle was here and all she had to do was march across the great ditch that had once been a moat, hammer on the doors and demand her rights. One hot bath.

'Just do it,' she told herself. 'Do it before you lose your nerve entirely.'

The massive gong echoed off the great stone walls as if in warning that an entire Viking war fleet was heading for the castle. Finn was half-way through his second coffee and the sound was enough to scare a man into the middle of next week. Or at least spill his coffee. 'What the…?'

'It's the doorbell, My Lord,' Mrs O'Reilly said placidly, heading out to the grand hall. 'It'll be the woman. If she's like her mother, heaven help us.' She tugged off her apron, ran her fingers through her permed grey hair, took a quick peep into one of the over-mantel mirrors and then tugged at the doors.

The oak doors swung open. And there was… Jo.

She was still in her bike gear but she must have washed. There wasn't a trace of mud on her, including her boots and trousers. Her face was scrubbed clean and she'd reapplied her make-up. Her kohl-rimmed eyes looked huge in her elfin face. Her cropped copper curls were combed and neat. She was smiling a wide smile, as if her welcome was assured.

He checked her legs and saw a telltale drip of water fall to her boots.

She was still sodden.

That figured. How many bikers had spare leathers in their kitbags?

She must be trying really hard not to shiver. He

looked back at the bright smile and saw the effort she was making to keep it in place.

'Good evening,' she was saying. She hadn't seen him yet. Mrs O'Reilly was at the door and he was well behind her. 'I hope I'm expected? I'm Jo Conaill. I'm very sorry I'm late. I had a small incident on the road.'

'You look just like your mother.' The warmth had disappeared from the housekeeper's voice as if it had never been. There was no disguising her disgust. The housekeeper was staring at Jo as if she was something the cat had just dragged in.

The silence stretched on—an appalled silence. Jo's smile faded to nothing. *What the...?*

Do something.

'Good evening to you too,' he said. He stepped forward, edging the housekeeper aside. He smiled at Jo, summoning his most welcoming smile.

And then there was even more silence.

Jo stared from Mrs O'Reilly to Finn and then back again. She looked appalled.

As well she might, Finn conceded. As welcomes went, this took some beating. She'd been greeted by a woman whose disdain was obvious, and by a man who'd seen her at her most vulnerable. Now

she was looking appalled. He thought of her reaction when he'd lifted her, carried her. She'd
seemed terrified and the look was still with her.

He thought suddenly of a deer he'd found on his
land some years back, a fawn caught in the ruins
of a disused fence. Its mother had run on his ap-
proach but the fawn was trapped, its legs tangled
in wire. It had taken time and patience to disen-
tangle it without it hurting itself in its struggles.

That was what this woman looked like, he
thought. Caught and wanting to run, but trapped.

She was so close to running.

Say something. 'We've met before.' He reached
out and took her hand. It was freezing. Wherever
she'd gone to get cleaned up, it hadn't been anywhere with a decent fire. 'I'm so glad you're...
clean.'

He smiled but she seemed past noticing.

'You live here?' she said with incredulity.

'This is Lord Finn Conaill, Lord of Castle Glenconaill,' the housekeeper snapped.

Jo blinked and stared at Finn as if she was expecting two heads. 'You don't look like a lord.'

'What do I look like?'

'A farmer. I thought you were a farmer.'

'I am a farmer. And you're an heiress.'

'I wait tables.'

'There you go. We've both been leading double lives. And now… It seems we're cousins?'

'You're not cousins,' Mrs O'Reilly snapped, but he ignored her.

'We're not,' he conceded, focusing only on Jo. 'Just distant relations. You should be the true heir to this whole place. You're the only grandchild.'

'She's illegitimate,' Mrs O'Reilly snapped and Finn moved a little so his body was firmly between Jo and the housekeeper. What was it with the woman?

'There's still some hereabouts who judge a child for the actions of its parents,' he said mildly, ignoring Mrs O'Reilly and continuing to smile down at Jo. 'But I'm not one of them. According to the lawyer, it seems you're Lord Conaill's granddaughter, marriage vows or not.'

'And…and you?' *What was going on?* She had the appearance of street-smart. She looked tough. But inside…the image of the trapped fawn stayed.

'My father was the son of the recently deceased Lord Conaill's cousin,' Finn told her. He furrowed his brows a little. 'I think that's right. I can't quite get my head around it. So that means my link to you goes back four generations. We're very distant relatives, but it seems we do share a great-great-grandfather. And the family name.'

'Only because of illegitimacy,' Mrs O'Reilly snapped.

Enough. He turned from Jo and faced Mrs O'Reilly square-on. She was little and dumpy and full of righteous indignation. She'd been Lord Conaill's housekeeper for years. Heaven knew, he needed her if he was to find his way around this pile but right now...

Right now he was Lord Conaill of Castle Glenconaill, and maybe it was time to assume his rightful role.

'Mrs O'Reilly, I'll thank you to be civil,' he said, and if he'd never had reason to be autocratic before he made a good fist of it now. He summoned all his father had told him of previous lords of this place and he mentally lined his ancestors up behind him. 'Jo's come all the way from Australia. She's inherited half of her grandfather's estate and for now this castle is her home. *Her* home. I therefore expect you to treat her with the welcome and the respect her position entitles her to. Do I make myself clear?'

There was a loaded silence. The housekeeper tried glaring but he stayed calmly looking at her, waiting, his face impassive. He was Lord of Glenconaill and she was his housekeeper. It was time she knew it.

Jo said nothing. Finn didn't look back at her but he sensed her shiver. If he didn't get her inside soon she'd freeze to death, he thought, but this moment was too important to rush. He simply stood and gazed down at Mrs O'Reilly and waited for the woman to come to a decision.

'I only...' she started but he shook his head.

'Simple question. Simple answer. Welcome and respect. Yes or no.'

'Her mother...'

'Yes or no!'

And finally she cracked. She took a step back but his eyes didn't leave hers. 'Yes.'

'Yes, what?' It was an autocratic snap. His great-great-grandfather would be proud of him, he thought, and then he thought of his boots and thought: *maybe not*. But the snap had done what he intended.

She gave a frustrated little nod, she bobbed a curtsy and finally she answered him as he'd intended.

'Yes, My Lord.'

What was she doing here? If she had to inherit a castle, why couldn't she have done it from a distance? She could have told the lawyer to put up a For Sale sign, sell it to the highest bidder and send her a cheque for half. Easy.

Why this insistence that she had to come?

Actually, it hadn't been insistence. It had been a strongly worded letter from the lawyer saying decisions about the entire estate had to be made between herself and this unknown sort-of cousin. It had also said the castle contained possessions that had been her mother's. The lawyer suggested that decisions would be easier to make with her here, and the estate could well afford her airfare to Ireland to make those decisions.

And it had been like a siren song, calling her... home?

No, that was dumb. This castle had never been her home. She'd never had a home but it was the only link she had to anyone. She might as well come and have a look, she'd thought.

But this place was like the bog that surrounded it. The surface was enticing but, underneath, it was a quagmire. The housekeeper's voice had been laced with malice.

Was that her mother's doing? Fiona? Well, maybe invective was to be expected. Maybe malice was deserved.

What hadn't been expected was this strong, hunky male standing in the doorway, taking her hand, welcoming her—and then, before her eyes, turning into the Lord of Glenconaill. Just like that. He'd been a solid Good Samaritan who'd pulled her out of the bog. He'd laughed at her—which she hadn't appreciated, but okay, he might have had reason—and then, suddenly, the warmth was gone and he was every bit a lord. The housekeeper was bobbing a curtsy, for heaven's sake. What sort of feudal system was this?

She was well out of her depth. She should get on her bike and leave.

But she was cold.

The lawyer had paid for her flight, for two nights' accommodation in Dublin and for the bike hire—he'd suggested a car or even a driver to meet her, but some things were non-negotiable. Two nights' accommodation and the bike was the extent of the largesse. The lawyer had assumed she'd spend the rest of her time in the castle, and she hadn't inherited anything yet. Plus the village had no accommodation and the thought of riding further was unbearable.

So, even if she'd like to ride off into the sunset, she wasn't in a position to do it.

Plus she was really, really cold.

Finn…Lord of Glenconaill?…was looking at her with eyes that said he saw more than he was letting on. But his gaze was kind again. The aristocratic coldness had disappeared.

His gaze dropped to the worn stone tiles. There was a puddle forming around her boots.

'I met Miss Conaill down the bog road,' he said, smiling at her but talking to the housekeeper. 'There were sheep on the road. Miss Conaill had struck trouble, was off her bike, wet and shaken, and I imagine she's still shaken.' He didn't say she'd been stuck in a bog, Jo thought, and a surge of gratitude made her almost light-headed. 'I offered to give her a ride but, of course, she didn't know who I was and I didn't know who she was. I expect that's why you're late, Miss Conaill, and I'm thinking you're still wet. Mrs O'Reilly, could you run Miss Conaill a hot bath, make sure her bedroom's warm and leave her be for half an hour? Then there's roast beef warm in the oven for you.'

His voice changed a little, and she could hear the return of the aristocrat. There was a firm threat to the housekeeper behind the words. 'Mrs O'Reilly will look after you, Jo, and she'll look after you well. When you're warm and fed, we'll talk again. Meanwhile, I intend to sit in your grandfather's study and see if I can start making sense of this pile we seem to have inherited. Mrs O'Reilly, I depend on you to treat Jo with kindness. This is her home.'

And there was nothing more to be said. The housekeeper took a long breath, gave an uncertain glance up at...her Lord?...and bobbed another curtsy.

'Yes, My Lord.'

'Let's get your gear inside,' Finn said. 'Welcome to Castle Glenconaill, Miss Conaill. Welcome to your inheritance.'

'There's no need for us to talk again tonight,' Jo managed. 'I'll have a bath and go to bed.'

'You'll have a bath and then be fed,' Finn said, and there was no arguing with the way he said it. 'You're welcome here, Miss Conaill, even if right now it doesn't feel like it.'

'Th…thank you,' she managed and turned to her bike to get her gear.

If things had gone well from there they might have been fine. She'd find her bedroom, have a bath, have something to eat, say goodnight and go to bed. She'd talk to the lawyer in the morning. She'd sign whatever had to be signed. She'd go back to Australia. That was the plan.

So far, things hadn't gone well for Jo, though, and they were about to get worse.

She had two bags—her kitbag with her clothes and a smaller one with her personal gear. She tugged them from the bike, she turned around and Finn was beside her.

He lifted the kitbag from her grasp and reached for the smaller bag. 'Let me.'

'I don't need help.'

'You're cold and wet and shaken,' he told her.

'It's a wise woman who knows when accepting help is sensible.'

This was no time to be arguing, she conceded, but she clung to her smaller bag and let Finn carry the bigger bag in.

He reached the foot of the grand staircase and then paused. 'Lead the way, Mrs O'Reilly,' he told the housekeeper, revealing for the first time that he didn't know this place.

And the housekeeper harrumphed and stalked up to pass them.

She brushed Jo on the way. Accidentally or on purpose, whatever, but it seemed a deliberate bump. She knocked the carryall out of Jo's hand.

And the bag wasn't properly closed.

After the bog, Jo had headed back to the village. She'd have loved to have booked a room at the pub but there'd been a No Vacancies sign in the porch, the attached cobwebs and dust suggesting there'd been no vacancies for years. She'd made do with a trip to the Ladies, a scrub under cold water—no hot water in this place—and an attempt at repair to her make-up.

She'd been freezing. Her hands had been shaking and she mustn't have closed her bag properly.

Her bag dropped now onto the ancient floor-boards of Castle Glenconaill and the contents spilled onto the floor.

They were innocuous. Her toiletries. The things she'd needed on the plane on the way over. Her latest project...

And it was this that the housekeeper focused on. There was a gasp of indignation and the woman was bending down, lifting up a small, clear plastic vial and holding it up like the angel of doom.

'I knew it,' she spat, turning to Jo with fury that must have been building for years. 'I knew how it'd be. Like mother, like daughter, and why your grandfather had to leave you half the castle... Your mother broke His Lordship's heart, so why you're here... What he didn't give her... She was nothing but a drug-addicted slut, and here you are, just the same. He's given you half his fortune and do you deserve it? How dare you bring your filthy stuff into this house?'

Finn had stopped, one boot on the first step. His brow snapped down in confusion. 'What are you talking about?'

'Needles.' The woman held up the plastic vial. 'You'll find drugs too, I'll warrant. Her mother couldn't keep away from the stuff. Dead from an overdose in the end, and here's her daughter just the same. And half the castle left to her... It breaks my heart.'

And Jo closed her eyes. *Beam me up*, she pleaded. Where was a time machine when she needed one? She'd come all this way to be tarred with the same brush as her mother. A woman she'd never met and didn't want to meet.

Like mother, like daughter... What a joke.

'I'll go,' she said in a voice she barely recognised. She'd sleep rough tonight, she decided. She'd done it before—it wouldn't kill her. Tomorrow she'd find the lawyer, sign whatever had to be signed and head back to Australia.

'You're going nowhere.' The anger in Finn's voice made her eyes snap open. It was a snap that reverberated through the ancient beams, from stone wall to stone wall, worthy of an aristocratic lineage as old as time itself. He placed the kitbag he was holding down and took the three steps to where the housekeeper was standing. He took the vial, stared at it and then looked at the housekeeper with icy contempt.

'You live here?' he demanded and the woman's fury took a slight dent.

'Of course.'

'Where?'

'I have an apartment...'

'Self-contained?'

'I...yes.'

'Good,' he snapped. 'Then go there now. Of all the cruel, cold welcomes...' He stared down at the vial and his mouth set in grim lines. 'Even if this was what you thought it was, your reaction would be unforgivable, but these are sewing needles. They have a hole at the end, not through the middle. Even if they were syringes, there's a score of reasons why Miss Conaill would carry them other than drug addiction. But enough. You're not to be trusted to treat Miss Conaill with common courtesy, much less kindness. Return to your apartment. I'll talk to you tomorrow morning but not before. I don't wish to see you again tonight. I'll take care of Miss Conaill. Go, now.'

'You can't,' the woman breathed. 'You can't tell me to go.'

'I'm Lord of Glenconaill,' Finn snapped. 'I believe the right is mine.'

Silence. The whole world seemed to hold its breath.

Jo stared at the floor, at her pathetic pile of toiletries and, incongruously, at the cover of the romance novel she'd read on the plane. It was historical, the Lord of the Manor rescuing and marrying his Cinderella.

Who'd want to be Cinderella? she'd thought as she read it, and that was what it felt like now. Cinderella should have options. She should be able to make the grand gesture, sweep from the castle in a flurry of skirts, say, *Take me to the nearest hostelry, my man, and run me a hot bath...*

A hot bath. There was the catch. From the moment Finn had said it, they were the words that had stuck in her mind. Everything else was white noise.

Except maybe the presence of this man. She was trying not to look at him.

The hero of her romance novel had been... romantic. He'd worn tight-fitting breeches and glossy boots and intricate neckcloths made of fine linen.

Her hero had battered boots and brawny arms and traces of copper in his deep brown hair. He looked tanned and weathered. His green eyes were creased by smiles or weather and she had no way of knowing which. He looked far too large to look elegant in fine linen and neckcloths, but maybe she was verging on hysterics because her mind had definitely decided it wanted a hero with battered boots. And a weathered face and smiley eyes.

Especially if he was to provide her with a bath.

'Go,' he said to Mrs O'Reilly and the woman cast him a glance that was half scared, half defiant. But the look Finn gave her back took the defiance out of her.

She turned and almost scuttled away, and Jo was left with Finn.

He didn't look at her. He simply bent and gathered her gear back into her bag.

She should be doing that. What was she doing, staring down at him like an idiot?

She stooped to help, but suddenly she was right at eye level, right…close.

His expression softened. He smiled and closed her bag with a snap.

'You'll be fine now,' he said. 'We seem to have routed the enemy. Let's find you a bath.'

And he rose and held out his hand to help her rise with him.

She didn't move. She didn't seem to be able to.

She just stared at that hand. Big. Muscled. Strong.

How good would it be just to put her hand in his?

'I forgot; you're a wary woman,' he said ruefully and stepped back. 'Very wise. I gather our ancestors have a fearsome reputation, but then they're your ancestors too, so that should make me wary as well. But if you can cope with me as a guide, I'll try and find you a bedroom. Mind, I've only just found my own bedroom but there seem to be plenty. Do you trust me to show you the way?'

How dumb was she being? Really dumb, she told herself, as well as being almost as offensive as the woman who'd just left. But still she didn't put her hand in his. Even though her legs were feeling like jelly—her feet were still icy—she managed to rise and tried a smile.

'Sorry. I...thank you.'

'There's no need to thank me,' he said ruefully. 'I had the warm welcome. I have no idea what bee

the woman has in her bonnet but let's forget her
and find you that bath.'

'Yes, please,' she said simply and thought, despite her wariness, if this man was promising her
a bath she'd follow him to the ends of the earth.

CHAPTER THREE

JO HAD A truly excellent bath. It was a bath she might well remember for the rest of her life.

Finn had taken her to the section of the castle where Mrs O'Reilly had allocated him a bedroom. He'd opened five doors, looking for another.

At the far end of the corridor, as far from Finn's as she could be, and also as far from the awesome bedroom they'd found by mistake—it had to have been her grandfather's—they'd found a small box room containing a single bed. It was the only other room with a bed made up, and it was obvious that was the room Mrs O'Reilly wanted her to use.

'We'll make up another,' Finn had growled in disgust—all the other rooms were better—but the bed looked good to Jo. Any bed would look good to Jo and when they'd found the bathroom next door and she'd seen the truly enormous bathtub she'd thought she'd died and gone to heaven.

So now she lay back, up to her neck in heat and steam. Her feet hurt when she got in, that was how cold they were, but the pain only lasted for moments and what was left was bliss.

She closed her eyes and tried to think of nothing at all.

She thought of Finn.

What manner of man was he? He was…what… her third cousin? Something removed? How did such things work? She didn't have a clue.

But they were related. He was…family? He'd defended her like family and such a thing had never happened to her.

He felt like…home.

And that was a stupid thing to think. How many times had she been sucked in by such sweetness?

'You're so welcome. Come in, sweetheart, let's help you unpack. You're safe here for as long as you need to stay.'

But it was never true. There was always a reason she had to move on.

She had to move on from here. This was a flying visit only.

To collect her inheritance? This castle must be

worth a fortune and it seemed her grandfather had left her half.

She had no idea how much castles were worth on the open market but surely she'd come out of it with enough to buy herself an apartment.

Or a Harley. That was a thought. She could buy a Harley and stay on the road for ever.

Maybe she'd do both. She could buy a tiny apartment, a place where she could crash from time to time when the roads got unfriendly. It didn't need to be big. It wasn't as if she had a lot of stuff.

Stuff. She opened her eyes and looked around her at the absurd, over-the-top bathroom. There was a chandelier hanging from the beams.

A portrait of Queen Victoria hung over the cistern, draped in a potted aspidistra.

Finn had hauled open the door and blanched. 'Mother of… You sure you want to use this?'

She'd giggled. After this whole appalling day, she'd giggled.

In truth, Finn Conaill was enough to make any woman smile.

'And that's enough of that,' she said out loud and splashed her face and then decided, dammit, splashing wasn't enough, she'd totally submerge. She did.

She came up still thinking of Finn.

He'd be waiting. 'Come and find me when you're dry and warm,' he'd said. 'There's dinner waiting for you somewhere. I may have to hunt to find it but I'll track it down.'

He would too, she thought. He seemed like a man who kept his promises.

Nice.

And Finn Conaill looked sexy enough to make a girl's toes curl. And when he smiled…

'Do Not Think About Him Like That!' She said it out loud, enunciating each word. 'You've been dumb enough for one day. Get tonight over with, get these documents signed and get out of here. Go buy your Harley.'

Harleys should be front and foremost in her mind. She'd never thought she'd have enough money to buy one and maybe now she would.

'So think about Harleys, not Finn Conaill,' she told herself as she reluctantly pulled the plug and let the hot water disappear. 'No daydreaming. You're dry and warm. Now, find yourself some dinner and go to bed. And keep your wits about you.'

But he's to be trusted, a little voice said.

But the old voice, the voice she knew, the only voice she truly trusted, told her she was being daft. *Don't trust anyone. Haven't you learnt anything by now?*

He heard her coming downstairs. Her tread was light but a couple of the ancient boards squeaked and he was listening for her.

He strode out to meet her and stopped and blinked.

She was wearing jeans and an oversized crimson sweater. She'd lost the make-up. Her face was a smatter of freckles and the rest seemed all eyes. She'd towelled her hair dry but it was still damp, the short curls tightly sprung, coiling as much as their length allowed.

She was wearing some kind of sheepskin bootees which looked massively oversized on her slight frame. She was flushed from the heat of her bath, and she looked like a kid.

She was treading down the stairs as if Here Be Dragons, and it was all he could do not to move forward and give her a hug of reassurance.

Right. As if that'd go down well. Earlier he'd

picked her up when she needed to be picked up and she'd pretty near had kittens.

He forced himself to stay still, to wait until she'd reached the bottom. Finally she looked around for where to go next and she saw him.

'Hey,' he said and smiled and she smiled back. It was a pretty good smile.

And that would be an understatement. This was the first time he'd seen this smile full on, and it was enough to take a man's breath away.

He had to struggle with himself to get his voice to sound prosaic.

'Kitchen?' he managed. 'Dining room's to the left if you like sitting with nineteen empty chairs and an epergne, or kitchen if you don't mind firestove and kettle.'

'Firestove and kettle,' she said promptly but peered left into the dining room, at its impressive size and its even more impressive—ostentatious?—furnishings. 'This is nuts. I have Queen Victoria in my bathroom. Medieval castle with interior decorator gone mad.'

'Not quite medieval, though the foundations might be. It's been built and rebuilt over the ages. According to Mrs O'Reilly, much of the current decorating was down to your mother. Apparently your grandfather kept to himself, the place gathered dust and when she was here she was bored.'

'Right,' she said dryly, looking askance at the suits of armour at the foot of the stairs. 'Are these guys genuine?'

'I've been looking at them. They're old enough, but there's not a scratch on them. Aren't they great?' He pointed to the sword blades. 'Note, though, that the swords have been tipped to make them safe. The Conaills of Glenconaill seem to have been into making money, not war. *To take and to hold* is their family motto.' He corrected himself. '*Our* family creed.'

'Not my creed,' she said dryly. 'I don't hold onto anything. Did you say dinner?'

'Kitchen this way. I used your bath time to investigate.' He turned and led her through thick wooden doors, into the kitchen beyond.

It was a truly impressive kitchen. A lord's kitchen.

A massive firestove set into an even larger hearth took up almost an entire wall. The floor was old stone, scrubbed and worn. The table was a vast slab of timber, scarred from generations of use.

The stove put out gentle heat. There was a rocker by the stove. Old calendars lined the walls as if it was too much trouble to take them down in the new year—simpler to put a new one up alongside. The calendars were from the local businesses, an eclectic mix of wildlife, local scenery and kittens. Many kittens.

Jo stopped at the door and blinked. 'Wow.'

'As you say, wow. Sit yourself down. Mrs O'Reilly said she'd kept your dinner hot.' He checked out the firestove, snagged a tea towel and opened the oven door.

It was empty. *What the heck?*

The firestove had been tamped for the night, the inlet closed. The oven was the perfect place to keep a dinner warm.

He closed the oven door and reconsidered. There was an electric range to the side—maybe for when the weather was too hot to use the firestove? Its light was on.

The control panel said it was on high.

He tugged open the oven door and found Jo's dinner. It was dried to the point where it looked inedible.

'Uh oh,' he said, hauling it out and looking at it

in disgust. And then he looked directly at Jo and decided to say it like it was. 'It seems our house-keeper doesn't like you.'

'She's never met me before tonight. I imagine it's that she doesn't...she didn't like my mother.'

'I'm sorry.'

'Don't be. I didn't like my mother myself. Not that I ever met her.'

He stared down at the dinner, baked hard onto the plate. Then he shrugged, lifted the lid of the trashcan and dumped the whole thing, plate and all, inside.

'You realise that's probably part of a priceless dinner set?' Jo said mildly.

'She wouldn't have served you on that. With the vitriol in the woman it's a wonder she didn't serve you on plastic. Sit down and I'll make you eggs and bacon. That is...' He checked the fridge and grinned. 'Eureka. Eggs and bacon. Would you like to tell me why no one seems to like your mother?'

'I'll cook.'

'No,' he said gently. 'You sit. You've come all the way from Australia and I've come from Kilkenny. Sit yourself down and be looked after.'

'You don't have to...'

'I want to, and eggs and bacon are my speciality.' He was already hauling things out of the fridge. 'Three eggs for you. A couple—no, make that three for me. It's been a whole hour since dinner, after all. Fried bread? Of course, fried bread, what am I thinking? And a side of fried tomato so we don't die of scurvy.'

So she sat and he cooked, and the smell of sizzling bacon filled the room. He focused on his cooking and behind him he sensed the tension seep from her. It was that sort of kitchen, he thought. Maybe they could pull the whole castle down and keep the kitchen. The lawyer had told him they needed to decide what to keep. This kitchen would be a choice.

'*To take and to hold.* Is that really our family creed?' Jo asked into the silence.

'*Accipere et Tenere.* It's over the front door. If my schoolboy Latin's up to it…'

'You did Latin in school?'

'Yeah, and me just a hayseed and all.'

'You're a hayseed?'

He didn't mind explaining. She was so nervous, it couldn't hurt to share a bit of himself.

'I have a farm near Kilkenny,' he told her. 'I

had a short, terse visit from your grandfather six months back, telling me I stood to inherit the title when he passed. Before that I didn't have a clue. Oh, I knew there was a lord way back in the family tree, but I assumed we were well clear of it. I gather our great grandfathers hated each other. The title and all the money went to your side. My side mostly starved in the potato famine or emigrated, and it sounded as if His Lordship thought we pretty much got what we deserved.'

He paused, thinking of the visit with the stooped and ageing aristocrat. Finn had just finished helping the team milk. He'd stood in the yard and stared at Lord Conaill in amazement, listening to the old man growl.

'He was almost abusive,' he told Jo now. 'He said, "Despite your dubious upbringing and low social standing, there's no doubt you'll inherit my ancient title. There's no one else. My lawyers tell me you're the closest in the male line. I can only pray that you manage not to disgrace our name." I was pretty much gobsmacked.'

'Wow,' Jo said. 'I'd have been gobsmacked too.' And then she stared at the plate he was putting down in front of her. 'Double wow. This is amazing.'

'Pretty impressive for a peasant.' He sat down with his own plate in front of him and she stared at the vast helping he'd given himself.

'Haven't you already eaten?'

'Hours ago.' At least one. 'And I was lambing at dawn.'

'So you really are a farmer.'

'Mostly dairy but I run a few sheep on the side. But I'll try and eat with a fork, just this once.' He grinned at her and then tackled his plate. 'So how about you? Has your grandfather been firing insulting directions at you too?'

'No.'

Her tone said, *Don't go there,* so he didn't. He concentrated on bacon.

It was excellent bacon. He thought briefly about cooking some more but decided it had to be up to Jo. Three servings was probably a bit much.

Jo seemed to focus on her food too. They ate in silence and he was content with that. Still he had that impression of nervousness. It didn't make sense but he wasn't a man to push where he wasn't wanted.

'Most of what I know of this family comes from one letter,' Jo said at last, and he nodded again and kept addressing his plate. He sensed information was hard to get from this woman. Looking up and seeming expectant didn't seem the way to get it.

'It was when I was ten,' she said at last. 'Addressed to my foster parents.'

'Your foster parents?'

'Tom and Monica Hastings. They were lovely. They wanted to adopt me. It had happened before, with other foster parents, but they never shared the letters.'

'I see.' Although he didn't. And then he thought, *Why not say it like it is?* 'You understand I'm from the peasant side of this family,' he told her. 'I haven't heard anything from your lot before your grandfather's visit, and that didn't fill me in on detail. So I don't know your history. I'd assumed I'd just be inheriting the title, and that only because I'm the next male in line, no matter how distant. Inheriting half this pile has left me stunned. It seems like it should all be yours, and yet here you are, saying you've been in foster homes...'

'Since birth.' Her tone was carefully neutral. 'Okay, maybe I do know a bit more than you, but not much. I was born in Sydney. My mother walked out of the hospital and left me there, giving my grandfather's name as the only person to contact. According to the Social Welfare notes that I've now seen—did you know you can get your file as an adult?—my grandfather was appalled at my very existence. His instructions were to have me adopted, get rid of me, but when my mother was finally tracked down she sent a curt letter back saying I wasn't for adoption; I was a Conaill, I was to stay a Conaill and my grandfather could lump it.'

'Your grandfather could lump it?'

'Yeah,' she said and rose and carried her plate to the sink. She ran hot water and started washing and he stood beside her and started wiping. It was an age-old domestic task and why it helped, he didn't know, but the action itself seemed to settle her.

'It seemed Fiona was a wild child,' she told him at last. 'She and my grandfather fought, and she seemed to do everything she could to shock him. If I'd been a boy I'm guessing she would have had him adopted. My grandfather might have valued a boy so having him adopted away from the family might have hurt him more than having an illegitimate grandchild. But I was just a girl so all she could do to shock him was keep me as a Conaill and grind it into his face whenever she could. So Social Welfare was left with him as first point of contact and I went from foster home to foster home. Because I'd been in foster care for ever, though, there was always the possibility of adoption. But every time any of my foster parents tried to keep me, they'd contact my grandfather and eventually he'd talk to Fiona—and she would refuse. It seemed she wanted to keep me in my grandfather's face.'

'So it was all about what was between Fiona and her father. Nothing about you.'

'It seems I was the tool to hurt him.' She shrugged and handed him the scrubbed frying pan. 'Nothing else. Why he's left me anything... I don't understand.'

'I suspect he ran out of options,' Finn told her. He kept his attention on the pan, not on her. 'I was the despised poor relation who stood to inherit the title whether he willed it to me or not. You were the despised illegitimate granddaughter. I imagine it was leave everything to us or leave it to a cats' home—and there's no sign that he was fond of cats.' He gazed around the kitten-adorned walls. 'Except in here, but I doubt the kitchen was his domain.'

'I guess.' She let the water run away and watched it swirl into the plughole. 'Isn't it supposed to swirl the other way?'

'What?'

'I'm in a different hemisphere. Doesn't the water go round in opposite directions?'

'What direction does it go round in Australia?'

'I have no idea.'

'You've never looked?'

'It's not the sort of thing you notice.'

'We could check it out on the Internet.'

'We could,' she conceded. 'Or we could go to bed.' And then she paused and flushed. 'I mean...' She stopped and bit her lip. 'I didn't...'

'You know, despite the fact that your mother was a wild child, I'm absolutely sure you didn't just proposition me,' he said gently and handed her the dishcloth to wipe her hands. 'You're tired, I'm tired and tomorrow we have a meeting with the lawyer and a castle to put on the market. That is, unless you'd like to keep it.'

She stared at him. 'Are you kidding? What would I do with a castle?'

'Exactly,' he said and took the dishcloth back from her and hung it up, then took her shoulders in his hands and twisted her and propelled her gently from the room. 'So tomorrow's for being sensible and we might as well start now. Bedtime, Jo Conaill. Don't dream of bogs.'

'I wouldn't dare,' she told him. 'I've been stuck in some pretty scary places in my time but the bog's the worst. Thank you for pulling me out.'

'It was my pleasure,' he told her. 'And Jo...'

'Yes?' He'd let her go. She was out of the door but glancing back at him.

'I'm glad I've inherited with you. If we have to be dissolute, unwanted relatives, it's good that it's two of us, don't you think?'

'I guess.' She frowned. 'I mean...we could have done this on our own.'

'But it wouldn't have been as much fun,' he told her. 'Tomorrow promises to be amazing. How many times in your life do you inherit a castle, Jo Conaill?' Then, as she didn't answer, he chuckled. 'Exactly. Mostly none. Go to bed, Jo, and sleep thinking of fun. Tomorrow you wake up as Lady of the Castle Glenconaill. If we have to inherit, why not enjoy it?'

'I'm not a Lady...'

'You could be,' he told her. 'Okay, neither of us belong, but tomorrow, just for a little, let's be Lord and Lady of all we survey. We might even Lord and Lady it over Mrs O'Reilly and if she gives us burnt toast for breakfast it's off with her head. What do you say?'

She gazed at him, dumbfounded, and then, slowly, her face creased into a smile again.

It really was a beautiful smile.

'Exactly,' he told her. 'Tomorrow this is our place. It's where we belong.'

'I don't belong.'

'Yes, you do,' he told her. 'Your grandfather and your mother no longer hold sway. Tomorrow you belong here.'

'I guess I could pretend...'

'There's no pretence about it. Tomorrow you belong right here.'

She met his gaze. Everything that needed to be said had been said but just for a moment she stayed. Just for a moment their gazes locked and something passed between... Something intan-

gible. Something strong and new and...unfath-
omable.

It was something he didn't understand and it
seemed she didn't either. She gazed at him for a
long moment and then she shook her head, as if
trying to clear a mist she'd never been in before.
As if trying to clear confusion.

'Goodnight,' she said in a voice that was decidedly unsteady.

'Goodnight,' he told her and finally she left.

He stood where he was.

Surely she hadn't guessed that he'd had a crazy
impulse to walk across and kiss her?

And surely her eyes hadn't said that that kiss
might have been welcome?

His bedroom was magnificent, almost as magnificent as the one the old Lord had slept in. He
lay in the vast four-poster bed and thought of the
cramped cots he and his brothers had shared as
kids, of the impoverished farm his parents had
struggled to keep, of a childhood lacking in anything but love.

But he thought of Jo and he knew he'd been
lucky. She'd told him little, and yet there was

so much behind her words that he could guess. A childhood of foster homes, and anyone who wanted to keep her being unable to do so.

She looked tough on the surface but he didn't need to scratch very deep before seeing scars.

She was...intriguing.

And that was something he shouldn't be thinking, he decided. Wasn't life complicated enough already?

'No.' He said it suddenly, out loud, and it surprised even him. His life wasn't complicated. He'd fought to make their parents' farm prosper. His father had died when he was in his teens and his brothers were younger. His mother had had no choice but to let him have his head. He'd set about changing things, firstly trying to keep them all from starving but in the end relishing the challenge. None of his brothers had had any inclination to stay on an impoverished farm. They'd gone on to have interesting, fulfilling careers but farming seemed to be in Finn's blood. By the time his mother died, twenty years later, the farm was an excellent financial concern.

And then there'd been Maeve, the girl next

door, the woman he'd always assumed shared his dreams. The woman he'd thought he'd marry.

'You're loyal to a fault.' Sean, his youngest brother, had thrown it at him on his last visit home. 'You took on the farm when you were little more than a kid and practically hauled us all up. You gave up your dreams for us. You never let our mam down. You've managed to make a go of the farm, and that's great, but Maeve—just because you promised eternal love when you were ten years old doesn't mean you owe her loyalty for life. She doesn't want this life. I'm thinking half what she thought was love for you was loyalty to her dad, but there's more to life than loyalty. She's seen it. So should you.'

Sean was right. The last twelve months had taught him that what he thought of as love was simply loyalty to a friend, loyalty to a way of life, loyalty to his vision of his future.

So where did his future lie now?

He thumped the pillow and then, when it didn't result in immediate sleep, he tossed back the covers and headed to the window. It was a vast casement window, the stone wall almost two feet thick.

Beneath the window the land of Glenconaill

stretched away to the moonlit horizon, miles of arable land reaching out to the bogs and then the mountains beyond.

If he'd inherited the whole thing…

'You didn't. This place is money only,' he muttered and deliberately drew the great velvet curtains closed, blocking out the night. 'Don't you be getting any ideas, Lord Finn of Glenconaill.'

And at the sound of his title he grinned. His brothers would never let him live it down. All now successful businessmen in their own rights, they'd think it was funny.

And Maeve…well, it no longer mattered what Maeve thought. He'd accepted it over the last few months and this morning's visit had simply confirmed it. Yes, she was in a mess but it wasn't a mess of his making. Their relationship was well over.

Had she faced her father or gone back to Dublin?

It was none of his business.

He headed back to bed and stared up at the dark and found himself thinking of the wide acres around Castle Glenconaill.

And a girl sleeping not so far from where he lay. A woman.

A woman named Jo.

By the time Jo came downstairs, the massive dining room was set up for breakfast. The housekeeper greeted her with a curt, 'Good morning, miss. Lord Conaill's in the dining room already. Would you like to start with coffee?'

It was pretty much your standard Bed and Breakfast greeting, Jo decided, and that was fine by her. Formal was good.

She walked into the dining room and Finn was there, reading the paper. He was wearing a casual shirt, sleeves rolled past his elbows. Sunbeams filtered through the massive windows at the end of the room. He looked up at her as she entered and he smiled, his deep green eyes creasing with pleasure at the sight of her—and it was all a woman could do not to gasp.

Where was formal when she needed it?

'Did you sleep well?' he asked and somehow she found her voice and somehow she made it work.

'How can you doubt it? Twelve hours!'

'So you'd be leaving the jet lag behind?'

'I hope so.' She sat at the ridiculous dining table and gazed down its length. Mrs O'Reilly had set places for them at opposite ends. 'We'll need a megaphone if we want to communicate.'

'Ah, but I don't think we're supposed to communicate. Formality's the order of the day. You're the aristocratic side of the family. I'm the peasant.'

'Hey, I'm on the wrong side of the blanket.'

'Then I'm under the bed, with the rest of the lint bunnies.'

She choked. The thought of this man as a lint bunny...

Mrs O'Reilly swept in then with coffee and placed it before her with exaggerated care. 'Mr O'Farrell's just phoned,' she told Finn, stepping back from the table and wiping her hands on her skirt as if she'd just done something dirty. 'He's the lawyer for the estate. He's been staying in Galway and he can be here in half an hour. I can ring him if that's not satisfactory.'

Finn raised his brows at Jo. 'Is that satisfactory with you?'

'I...yes.'

'We can see him then,' Finn told her. 'In Lord Conaill's study, please. Could you light the fire?'

'The drawing room would be…'

'The study, please,' Finn said inexorably and the woman stared at him.

Finn gazed calmly back. Waiting.

For a moment Jo thought she wouldn't answer. Finally she gave an angry tut and nodded.

'Yes, My Lord.'

'Mrs O'Reilly?'

'Yes.'

'You haven't asked Miss Conaill what she'd like for breakfast.'

'Toast,' Jo said hurriedly.

'And marmalade and a fruit platter,' Finn added. 'And I trust it'll be up to the excellent standard you served me. You do realise you burned Miss Conaill's dinner last night?'

He was holding the woman's gaze, staring her down, and with a gaze like that there was never any doubt as to the outcome.

'I'm sorry, My Lord. It won't happen again.'

'It won't,' Finn told her and gave a curt nod and went back to his newspaper.

The woman disappeared. Jo gazed after her with awe and then turned back to Finn. He was watching her, she found. He'd lowered his paper and was smiling at her, as if giving the lie to the gruff persona she'd just witnessed.

And it was too much. She giggled. 'Where did you learn to be a lord?' she demanded. 'Or is that something that's born into you with the title?'

'I practice on cows,' he said with some pride. 'I've had six months to get used to this Lordship caper. The cows have been bowing and scraping like anything.' He put his paper down and grinned. 'Not my brothers so much,' he admitted. 'They haven't let me live it down since they heard. Insubordination upon insubordination. You've never seen anything like it.'

'Do you guys share the farm?' She held her coffee, cradling its warmth. The dining room had an open fire in the hearth, the room was warm enough, but the sheer size of it was enough to make her shiver.

'I own my parents' farm outright, but it wasn't much of an inheritance when I started. My brothers all left for what they saw as easier careers and they've done well. Me? I've put my heart and soul into the farm and it's paid off.'

'You're content?'

He grinned at that. 'I'm a lord. How can I not be content?'

'I meant with farming.'

'Of course I am. I don't need a castle to be content. Cows are much more respectful than house-keepers.'

'I'm sure they are,' she said, thinking the man was ridiculous. But she kind of liked it.

She kind of liked him.

'No wife and family?' she asked, not that it was any of her business but she might as well ask.

'No.' He shrugged and gave a rueful smile. 'I've had a long-term girlfriend who's recently decided long-term is more than long enough. See me suffering from a broken heart.'

'Really?'

'Not really.' He grinned. 'I'll live.'

And then Mrs O'Reilly came sniffing back in with toast and he followed her every move with an aristocratically raised eyebrow until she disappeared again. It was a bit much for Jo.

'You do the Lord thing beautifully.'

'You should try.'

'Not me. I'm inheriting what there is to inherit and then I'm out of here.'

'Maybe that's wise,' Finn said thoughtfully. 'From all accounts, your grandpa wasn't the happiest of men. Maybe being aristocratic isn't all it's cut out to be.'

'But being content is,' she said softly. 'I'm glad…I'm glad, Finn Conaill, that you're content.'

The lawyer arrived just as Mrs O'Reilly finished clearing breakfast. Jo had had half a dozen emails from this man, plus a couple of phone calls from his assistant. She'd checked him out on the Internet. He was a partner in a prestigious Dublin law firm. She expected him to be crusty, dusty and old.

He turned up in bike leathers. He walked in, blond, blue-eyed, his helmet tucked under one arm, a briefcase by his side, and she found herself smiling as she stood beside Finn to greet him. There were things she'd been dreading over this meeting. Being intimidated by the legal fraternity was one of them, but this guy was smiling back at her, dumping his gear, holding out his hand in greeting. A fellow biker.

'Whose is the bike?' he asked.

'Mine,' she said. 'Hired in Dublin.'

'You should have let me know. My father would disapprove but I know a place that hires vintage babies. Or there are places that hire Harleys. We could have set one up for you.'

'You're kidding. A Harley?' She couldn't disguise the longing.

'No matter. After this morning, I imagine you'll be able to buy half a dozen Harleys.' He glanced at Finn and smiled. 'And yours will be the Jeep?'

And there it was, the faintest note of condescension. Jo got it because she was used to it, and she glanced up at Finn's face and she saw he got it too. And his face said he was used to it as well.

The lawyer's accent was strongly English. She'd read a bit of Ireland's background before she came. The lawyer would be public school educated, she thought. Finn...not so much. But she watched his face and saw the faint twitch at the edges of his mouth, the deepening of the creases at his eyes and thought, *He's amused by it.*

And she thought, *You'd be a fool to be condescending to this man.*

'I'm the Jeep,' he conceded.

'And the new Lord Conaill of Glenconaill,' the

lawyer said and held out his hand. 'Congratulations. You're a lucky man.'

'Thank you,' Finn said gravely. 'I'm sure every Irishman secretly longs for his very own castle. I might even need to learn to eat with a fork to match.'

He grinned to take any offence from the words and Jo found herself grinning back. This man got subtle nuances, she thought, but, rather than bristling, he enjoyed them. She looked from Finn to the lawyer and thought this farmer was more than a match for any smart city lawyer.

'Lord Conaill and I have just been having breakfast,' she said. 'Before he takes me on a tour of the estate.'

'You know you're sharing?'

'And that's what you need to explain,' Finn said and they headed into her grandfather's study, where John O'Farrell of O'Farrell, O'Farrell and O'Lochlan spent an hour explaining the ins and outs of their inheritance.

Which left Jo…gobsmacked.

She was rich. The lawyer was right. If she wanted, she could have half a dozen Harleys. Or much, much more.

The lawyer had gone through each section of the estate, explaining at length. She'd tried to listen. She'd tried to take it in but the numbers were too enormous for her to get her head around. When he finally finished she sat, stunned to silence, and Finn sat beside her and she thought, *He's just as stunned as I am.*

Unbelievable.

'So it's straight down the middle,' Finn said at last. 'One castle and one fortune.'

'That's right and, on current valuations, they're approximately equal. In theory, one of you could take the castle, the other the fortune that goes with it.' The lawyer looked at Jo and smiled. He'd been doing that a bit, not-so-subtle flirting. But then he decided to get serious again and addressed Finn.

'However, if you did have notions of keeping the castle, of setting yourself up as Lord of Glenconaill and letting Miss Conaill take the rest, I have bad news. This place is a money sink. My father has been acting as financial adviser to Lord Conaill for the last forty years and he knows how little has been spent on the upkeep of both castle and land. He's asked me to make sure you know it. The cosmetic touches have been done—Lord

Conaill was big on keeping up appearances and his daughter insisted on things such as central heating—but massive capital works are needed to keep this place going into the future. Lord Conaill told my father he thought your own farm is worth a considerable amount but, in my father's opinion, if you wished to keep the castle, you'd need considerably more. And, as for Miss Conaill...' he smiled again at Jo '...I suspect this lady has better things to do with a fortune than sink it into an ancient castle.'

Did she?

A fortune...

What would the likes of her do with a fortune?

Finn wasn't speaking. He'd turned and was looking out of the massive casement window to the land beyond.

He'd need time to take this in, she thought. They both would. This was...massive. She tried to think of how it would affect her, and couldn't. She tried to think of how it would affect Finn, but watching his broad shoulders at the window was making things seem even more disconcerting.

So focus on something else. Anything.

'What about Mrs O'Reilly?' she found herself asking, and the lawyer frowned.

'What about her?'

'It's just...there's no mention of her in the will and she seems to have been here for ever. She knew my mother.'

Finn turned and stared at her. She kept looking at the lawyer.

'I believe she has,' the lawyer said. 'There has been...discussion.'

'Discussion?'

'She rang after the funeral,' the lawyer admitted. 'Her husband was the old Lord's farm manager and she's maintained the castle and cared for your grandfather for well over thirty years. My father believes she's been poorly paid and overworked—very overworked as the old Lord wouldn't employ anyone else. My father believes she stayed because she was expecting some sort of acknowledgement in the will. She knew the castle was to be left to you, My Lord,' he told Finn. 'But it would have been a shock to hear the remainder was to be left to a granddaughter he'd never seen.'

He hesitated then but finally decided to tell

it how it was. 'The old Lord wasn't without his faults,' he told them. 'My father said he wouldn't be surprised if he'd made promises to her that he had no intention of keeping. It gave him cheap labour.'

'And now?' Jo asked in a small voice.

'Her husband died last year. The place is without a farm manager and I wouldn't imagine you'll be having ongoing use for a housekeeper. She'll move out as soon as you wish.'

'But she's been left nothing? No pension? Nothing at all?'

'No.'

'That sucks,' Jo said.

'She doesn't like you,' Finn reminded her, frowning.

'It still sucks. She took care of my grandfather?'

'I believe she did,' the lawyer told her. 'For the last couple of months he was bedbound and she nursed him.'

'And she hated my mother, so she can't be all bad. How much would a cottage in the village and a modest pension be? Actually, you don't even need to tell me. Work it out and take it from my half.'

'She burned your dinner!' Finn expostulated.

Jo shrugged and smiled. 'If I thought she'd just inherited my home I might have burned her dinner.'

'She called your mother a drug addict.'

'My mother *was* a drug addict.' She turned back to the lawyer. 'Can you set it up?'

'Of course, but...'

'Take it from both sides,' Finn growled. 'We both have a responsibility towards her and we can afford to be generous. A decent house and a decent pension.'

'There's no need...' Jo started.

'We're in this together,' he said.

The lawyer nodded. 'It seems reasonable. A pension and a local cottage for Mrs O'Reilly will scarcely dent what you'll inherit.

'Well, then,' he said, moving on. 'Irish castles with a history as long as this sell for a premium to overseas buyers looking for prestige. If you go through the place and see if there's anything you wish to keep, we can include everything else with the sale. I'd imagine you don't wish to stay here any longer than you need. Would a week to sort things out be enough? Make a list of anything you wish to keep, and then I'll come back with staff and start cataloguing. You could both have your inheritance by Christmas.' He smiled again at Jo. 'A Harley for Christmas?'

'That'd be…good,' Jo said with a sideways look at Finn. How did he feel about this? She felt completely thrown.

'Excellent,' Finn said and she thought he felt the same as she did.

How did she know? She didn't, she conceded. She was guessing. She was thinking she knew this man, but on what evidence?

'Jo, let me know when you've finished up here,' the lawyer was saying. 'We can advance you money against the estate so you can stay somewhere decent in Dublin. I can lend you one of my bikes. I could take you for a ride up to Wicklow, show you the sights. Take you somewhere decent for dinner.'

'Thanks,' she said, though she wasn't all that sure she wanted to go anywhere with this man, with his slick looks and his slick words.

'And you'll be imagining all the cows you can buy,' he said jovially to Finn and she saw Finn's lips twitch again.

'Eh, that'd be grand. Cows…I could do with a

few of those. I might need to buy myself a new bucket and milking stool to match.'

He was laughing but the lawyer didn't get it. He was moving on. 'Welcome to your new life of wealth,' he told them. 'Now, are you both sure about Mrs O'Reilly?'

'Yes.' They spoke together, and Finn's smile deepened. 'It's a good idea of Jo's.'

'Well, I may just pop into the kitchen and tell her,' the lawyer told them. 'I know she's been upset and, to be honest, my father was upset on her behalf.'

'But you didn't think to tell us earlier?' Finn demanded.

'It's not my business.' He shrugged. 'What you do with your money is very much your own business. You can buy as many milking stools as you want. After the castle's sold I expect I won't see you again. Unless...' He smiled suggestively at Jo. 'Unless you decide to spend some time in Dublin.'

'I won't,' Jo said shortly and he nodded.

'That's fine. Then we'll sell this castle and be done with it.'

CHAPTER FOUR

WHAT HAD JUST happened seemed too big to get
their heads around. They farewelled the lawyer.
They looked at each other.

'How many people do you employ on your
farm?' Jo asked and he smiled. He'd enjoyed the
lawyer's attempt at condescension and he liked
that Jo had too.

'Ten, at last count.'

'That's a lot of buckets.'

'It is and all.'

'Family?' she asked.

'My parents are dead and my brothers have
long since left.' He could tell her about Maeve,
he thought, but then—why should he? Maeve was
no longer part of his life.

'So there's just you and a huge farm.'

'Yes.'

'But you're not wealthy enough to buy me out?'

He grinned at that. 'Well, no,' he said apologetically. 'Didn't you hear our lawyer? He already has it figured.'

He tried smiling again, liking the closeness it gave them, but Jo had closed her eyes. She looked totally blown away.

'I need a walk.'

And he knew she meant by herself. He knew it because he needed the same. He needed space to get his head around the enormity of what had just happened. So he nodded and headed outside, across the castle grounds, past the dilapidated ha-ha dividing what had once been gardens from the fields beyond, and then to the rough ground where sheep grazed contentedly in the spring sunshine.

The lawyer's visit had thrown him more than he cared to admit, and it had thrown him for two reasons.

One was the sheer measure of the wealth he stood to inherit.

The second was Jo. Her reaction to Mrs O'Reilly's dilemma had blown him away. Her generosity...

Also the smarmy lawyer's attempt to flirt with

her. Finn might have reacted outwardly to the lawyer with humour but inwardly...

Yeah, inwardly he'd have liked to take that smirk off the guy's face and he wouldn't have minded how he did it.

Which was dumb. Jo was a good-looking woman. It was only natural that the lawyer had noticed and what happened between them was nothing to do with Finn.

So focus on the farm, he told himself, but he had to force himself to do it.

Sheep.

The sheep looked scrawny. How much had their feed been supplemented during the winter? he asked himself, pushing all thoughts of Jo stubbornly aside, and by the time he'd walked to the outer reaches of the property he'd decided: not at all.

The sheep were decent stock but neglected. Yes, they'd been shorn but that seemed to be the extent of animal husbandry on the place. There were rams running with the ewes and the rams didn't look impressive. It seemed no one really cared about the outcome.

There were a couple of cows in a small field

near the road. One looked heavily in calf. House cows? He couldn't imagine Mrs O'Reilly adding milking to her duties and both were dry. The cows looked as scrawny as the landscape.

Back home in Kilkenny, the grass was shooting with its spring growth. The grass here looked starved of nutrients. It'd need rotation and fertiliser to keep these fields productive and it looked as if nothing had been done to them for a very long time.

He kept walking, over the remains of ancient drainage, long blocked.

Would some American or Middle Eastern squillionaire pay big bucks for this place? He guessed they would. They'd buy the history and the prestige and wouldn't give a toss about drainage.

And it wasn't their place. It was...*his*?

It wasn't, but suddenly that was the way he felt.

This was nuts. How could he feel this way about a place he hadn't seen before yesterday?

He had his own farm and he loved it. His brothers had grown and moved on but he'd stayed. He loved the land. He was good at farming and the farm had prospered in his care. He'd pushed boundaries. He'd built it into an excellent commercial success.

But this... Castle Glenconaill... He turned to look at its vast silhouette against the mountains and, for some reason, it almost felt as if it was part of him. His grandfather must have talked of it, he thought, or his father. He couldn't remember, but the familiarity seemed bone-deep.

He turned again to look out over the land. What a challenge.

To take and to hold...

The family creed seemed wrong, he decided, but *To hold and to honour...* That seemed right. To take this place and hold its history, to honour the land, to make this place once more a proud part of Irish heritage... If he could do that...

What was he thinking? He'd inherited jointly with a woman from Australia. Jo had no reason to love this place and every reason to hate it. And the lawyer was right; even with the wealth he now possessed, on his own he had no hope of keeping it. To try would be fantasy, doomed to disaster from the start.

'So sell it and get over it,' he told himself, but

the ache to restore this place, to do something, was almost overwhelming.

He turned back to the castle but paused at the ha-ha. The beautifully crafted stone wall formed a divide so stock could be kept from the gardens without anything as crass as a fence interfering with the view from the castle windows. But in places the wall was starting to crumble. He looked at it for a long moment and then he couldn't resist. Stones had fallen. They were just…there.

He knelt and started fitting stone to stone.

He started to build.

To hold and to honour… He couldn't hold, he decided, but, for the time he was here, he would do this place honour.

Jo thought about heading outside but Finn had gone that way and she knew he'd want to be alone. There was silence from the kitchen. Mrs O'Reilly was either fainting from shock or trying to decide whether she could tell them they could shove their offer. Either way, maybe she needed space too.

Jo started up towards her bedroom and then, on impulse, turned left at the foot of the staircase instead of going up.

Two massive doors led to what looked like an ancient baronial hall. She pushed the doors open and stopped dead.

The hall looked as if it hadn't been used for years. Oversized furniture was draped with dustsheets and the dustsheets themselves were dusty. Massive beams ran the length of the hall, and up in the vaulted ceiling hung generations of spider webs. The place was cold and dank and...amazing.

'Like something out of Dickens,' she said out loud and her voice echoed up and up. She thought suddenly of Miss Havisham sitting alone in the ruins of her bridal finery and found herself grinning.

She could rent this place out for Halloween parties. She could...

Sell it and go home.

Home? There was that word again.

And then her attention was caught. On the walls...tapestries.

Lots of tapestries.

When she'd first entered she'd thought they were paintings but now, making her way cautiously around the edges of the hall, she could make out scores of needlework artworks. Some were small. Some were enormous.

They were almost all dulled, matted with what must have been smoke from the massive blackened fireplace at the end of the room. Some were frayed and damaged. All were amazing.

She fingered the closest and she was scarcely breathing.

It looked like...life in the castle? She recognised the rooms, the buildings. It was as if whoever had done the tapestries had set themselves the task of recording everyday life in the castle. Hunting. Formal meals with scores of overdressed guests. Children at play. Dogs...

She walked slowly round the room and thought, *These aren't from one artist and they're not from one era.*

They were the recording of families long gone.

Her family? Her ancestors?

It shouldn't make a difference but suddenly it did. She hated that they were fading, splitting, dying.

Her history...

And Finn's, she thought suddenly. In her great-great-grandfather's era, they shared a heritage.

Maybe she could take them back to Sydney and restore them.

Why? They weren't hers. They'd be bought by whoever bought this castle.

They wouldn't be her ancestors, or Finn's ancestors. They'd belong to the highest bidder.

Maybe she could keep them.

But Jo didn't keep *stuff*, and that was all these were, she reminded herself. *Stuff.* But still… She'd restored a few tapestries in the past and she wasn't bad at it. She knew how to do at least step one.

As she'd crossed the boundaries of the castle last night she'd crossed a creek. No, a stream, she corrected herself. Surely in Ireland they had streams. Or burns? She'd have to ask someone.

But meanwhile it was spring, and the mountains above Castle Glenconaill must surely have been snow-covered in winter. The stream below the castle seemed to be running full and free. Clear, running water was the best way she knew to get soot and stains from tapestries, plumping up the threads in the process.

She could try with a small one, she decided, as her fingers started to itch. She'd start with one of the hunting scenes, a brace of pheasants without people or place. That way, if she hurt it, it wouldn't matter. She could start with that one and…

And nothing. She was going home. Well, back to Australia.

Yeah, she was, but first she was getting excited. First, she was about to clean a tapestry.

Finn had placed a dozen rocks back in their rightful position and was feeling vaguely pleased with himself. He'd decided he should return to the castle to see what Jo was doing—after all, they were here for a purpose and repairing rock walls wasn't that purpose—and now here she was, out in the middle of the stream that meandered along the edge of the ha-ha.

What was she doing? Those rocks were slippery. Any minute now she'd fall and get a dunking.

'Hey!'

She looked up and wobbled, but she didn't fall. She gave him a brief wave and kept on doing what she was doing.

Intrigued, he headed over to see.

She was messing with something under water. The water would be freezing. She had the sleeves of her sweater pulled up and she'd hauled off her shoes. She was knee-deep in water.

'What's wrong?'

She kept concentrating, her back to him, stooped, as if adjusting something under water. He stood and waited, more and more intrigued, until finally she straightened and started her unsteady way back to the shore.

'Done.'

He could see green slime attached to the rocks underneath the surface. She was stepping gingerly from rock to rock but even the ones above the surface would be treacherous.

He took a couple of steps out to help her—and slipped himself, dunking his left foot up to his ankle.

He swore.

'Whoops,' Jo said and he glanced up at her and she was grinning. 'Uh oh. I'm sorry. I'd carry you if I could but I suspect you're a bit heavy.'

'What on earth are you doing?'

'Heading back to the castle. All dry.' She reached the shore, jumping nimbly from the last rock, then turned and proffered a hand to him. 'Can I help?'

'No,' he said, revolted, and her smile widened.

'How sexist is that? Honestly...'

'I was trying to help.'

'There's been a bit of that about,' she said. 'It's not that I don't appreciate it; it's just that I hardly ever need it. Bogs excepted.'

'What were you doing?' He hauled himself out of the water to the dry bank and surveyed his leg in disgust. His boot would take ages to dry. Jo, on the other hand, was drying her feet with a sock and tugging her trainers back on. All dry.

'Washing tapestries,' she told him and he forgot about his boots.

'Tapestries...?'

'The hall's full of them. You should see. They're awesome. But they're filthy and most of them need work. I've brought one of the small ones here to try cleaning.'

'You don't think,' he asked cautiously, 'that soap and water might be more civilised?'

'Possibly. But not nearly as much fun.'

'Fun...' He stared at his leg and she followed his gaze and chuckled.

'Okay, fun for me, not for you. I'm obviously better at creeks than you are.'

'Creeks...'

'Streams. Brooks. What else do you call them? Whatever, they'll act just the same as home.' She gestured to the surrounding hills, rolling away to the mountains in the background. 'Spring's the best time. The water's pouring down from the hills; it's running fast and clean and it'll wash through tapestries in a way nothing else can, unless I'm prepared to waste a day's running water in the castle. Even then, I wouldn't get an even wash.'

'So you just lie it in the stream.' He could see it now, a square of canvas, stretched underwater and weighed down by rocks at the edges.

'The running water removes dust, soot, smoke and any burnt wool or silk. It's the best way. Some people prefer modern cleaning methods, but in my experience they can grey the colours. And, as well, this way the fibres get rehydrated. They plump up almost as fat as the day they were stitched.'

'You're intending to leave it here?'

'I'll bring it in tonight. You needn't worry; I'm not about to risk a cow fording the stream and sticking a hoof through it.'

'And then what will you do?' he asked, fascinated.

'Let it dry and fix it, of course. This one's not bad. It has a couple of broken relays and warps but nothing too serious. I'll see how it comes up after cleaning but I imagine I'll get it done before I leave. How's the stone wall going?'

To say he was dumbfounded would be an understatement. This woman was an enigma. Part of her came across tough; another part was so fragile he knew she could break. She was wary, she seemed almost fey, and here she was calmly setting about restoring tapestries as if she knew exactly what she was talking about.

He was sure she did.

'You saw me working?' he managed and she nodded.

'I walked past and you didn't see me. It feels good, doesn't it, working on something you love. So…half a yard of wall fixed, three or four hundred yards to go? Reckon you'll be finished in a week?' She clambered nimbly up the bank and turned and offered a hand. 'Need a pull?'

'No,' he said, and she grinned and withdrew her hand.

And he missed it. He should have just taken it. If he had she would have tugged and he would have ended up right beside her. Really close.

But she was smiling and turning to head back to the castle and it was dumb to feel a sense of opportunity lost.

What was he thinking? Life was complicated enough without feeling…what he was feeling…

And that's enough of that, he told himself soundly. It behoved a man to take a deep breath and get himself together. This woman was…complicated, and hadn't he decided on the safe option in life? His brothers had all walked off the land to make their fortunes and they'd done well. But Finn… He'd stayed and he'd worked the land he'd inherited. He'd aimed for a good farm on fertile land. A steady income. A steady woman?

Like Maeve. That was a joke. He'd thought his dreams were her dreams. He'd known her since childhood and yet it seemed he hadn't known her at all.

So how could he think he knew Jo after less than a day?

And why was he wondering how he could know her better?

'So do you intend to keep the suits of armour?' Jo asked and he struggled to haul his thoughts back to here and now. Though actually they were here and now. They were centred on a slip of a girl in a bright crimson sweater and jeans and stained trainers.

If Maeve had come to the castle with him, she'd have spent a week shopping for clothes in preparation.

But his relationship with Maeve was long over—apart from the minor complication that she wouldn't tell her father.

The sun was on his face. Jo was by his side, matching his stride even though her legs were six inches shorter than his. She looked bright and interested and free.

Of course she was free. She was discussing the fate of two suits of armour before she climbed back on her bike and headed back to Australia.

'I can't see them back on the farm,' he admitted.

'Your farm is somewhere near a place called Kilkenny,' she said. 'So where is that? You head down to Tipperary and turn…?'

'North-east. I don't go that way. But how do you know of Tipperary?'

'I looked it up on the map when I knew I was coming. There's a song… *It's a Long Way to Tipperary*. I figured that's where I was coming. A long way. And you farm cows and sheep?'

'The dairy's profitable but I'd like to get into sheep.'

'It's a big farm?'

'Compared to Australian land holdings, no. But it's very profitable.'

'And you love it.'

Did he love it?

As a kid he certainly had, when the place was rundown, when everywhere he'd looked there'd been challenges. But now the farm was doing well and promising to do better. With the money from the castle he could buy properties to the north.

If he wanted to.

'It's a great place,' he said mildly. 'How about you? Do you work at what you love?'

'I work to fund what I love.'

'Which is?'

'Tapestry and motorbikes.'

'Tell me about tapestry,' he said, and she looked a bit defensive.

'I didn't just look up the Internet and decide to

restore from Internet Lesson 101. I've been playing with tapestries for years.'

'Why?' It seemed so unlikely...

'When I was about ten my then foster mother gave me a tapestry do-it-yourself kit. It was a canvas with a painting of a cat and instructions and the threads to complete it. I learned the basics on that cat, but when I finished I thought the whiskers looked contrived. He also looked smug so I ended up unpicking him a bit and fiddling. It started me drawing my own pictures. It works for me. It makes me feel...settled.'

'So what do you do the rest of the time?'

'I make coffee. Well. I can also wait tables with the best of them. It's a skill that sees me in constant work.'

'You wouldn't rather work with tapestries?'

'That'd involve training to be let near the decent ones, and training's out of my reach.'

'Even now you have a massive inheritance?'

She paused as if the question took concentration. She stared at her feet and then turned and gazed out at the grounds, to the mountains beyond.

'I don't know,' she admitted. 'I like café work. I like busy. It's kind of like a family.'

'Do they know where you are?'

'Who? The people I work with?'

'Yes.'

'Do you mean if I'd sunk in a bog yesterday would they have cared or even known?' She shrugged. 'Nope. That's not what I mean by family. I pretty much quit work to come here. Someone's filling in for me now, but I'll probably just get another job when I go back. I don't stay in the same place for long.'

'So when you said family…'

'I meant people around me. It's all I want. Cheerful company and decent coffee.'

'And you're stuck here with me and Mrs O'Reilly and coffee that tastes like mud.'

'You noticed,' she said approvingly. 'That's a start.'

'A start of what?' he asked mildly and she glanced sharply up at him as if his question had shocked her. Maybe it had. He'd surprised himself—it wasn't a question he'd meant to ask and he wasn't sure what exactly he was asking.

But the question hung.

'I guess the start of nothing,' she said at last with

a shrug that was meant to be casual but didn't quite come off. 'I can cope with mud coffee for a week.'

'All we need to do is figure what we want to keep.'

'I live out of a suitcase. I can't keep anything.' She said it almost with defiance.

'And the armour wouldn't look good in a nice modern bungalow.'

'Is that what your farmhouse is?'

'It is.' The cottage he'd grown up in had long since deteriorated past repair. He'd built a large functional bungalow.

It had a great kitchen table. The rest...yeah, it was functional.

'I saw you living somewhere historic,' Jo said. 'Thatch maybe.'

'Thatch has rats.'

She looked up towards the castle ramparts. 'What about battlements? Do battlements have rats?'

'Not so much.' He grinned. 'Irish battlements are possibly a bit cold even for the toughest rat.'

'What about you, Lord Conaill? Too cold for you?'

'I'm not Lord Conaill.'

'All the tapestries in the great hall...they're

mostly from a time before your side of the family split. This is your history too.'

'I don't feel like Lord Conaill.'

'No, but you look like him. Go in and check the tapestries. You have the same aristocratic nose.'

He put his hand on his nose. 'Really?'

'Yep. As opposed to mine. Mine's snub with freckles, not an aristocratic line anywhere.'

And he looked at her freckles and thought... it might not be the Conaill nose but it was definitely cute.

He could just...

Not. How inappropriate was it to want to reach out and touch a nose? To trace the line of those cheekbones.

To touch.

He knew enough about this woman to expect a pretty firm reaction. Besides, the urge was ridiculous. Wasn't it?

'I reckon your claim to the castle's a lot stronger than mine,' she was saying and he had to force his attention from her very cute nose to what they were talking about.

They'd reached the forecourt. He turned and faced outward, across the vast sweep of Glenconaill to the mountains beyond. It was easier talking about abstracts when he wasn't looking at the reality of her nose. And the rest of her.

'Your grandfather left the castle to two strangers,' he told her. 'We're both feeling as if we have no right to be here, and yet he knew I was to inherit the title. He came to my farm six months ago and barked the information at me, yet there was never an invitation to come here. And you were his granddaughter and he didn't know you either. He knew we'd stand here one day, but he made no push to make us feel we belong. Yet we do belong.'

'You feel that?'

'I don't know,' he said slowly. 'It's just…walking across the lands today, looking at the sheep, at the ruined walls, at the mess this farmland has become, it seems a crime that no push was made…'

'To love it?' She nodded. 'I was thinking that. The tapestries… A whole family history left to disintegrate.' She shrugged. 'But we can't.'

'I guess not.' He gazed outward for a long moment, as though soaking in something he needed to hold to. 'Of course you're right.'

'If he'd left it all to you, you could have,' Jo said and he shrugged again.

'Become a Lord in fact? Buy myself ermine robes and employ a valet?'

'Fix a few stone walls?'

'That's more tempting,' he said and then he grinned. 'So your existence has saved me from a life of chipping at cope stones. Thank you, Jo. Now, shall we find out if Mrs O'Reilly intends to feed us?'

And Jo thought…it felt odd to walk towards Castle Glenconaill with this man by her side.

But somehow, weirdly, it felt right.

'What are you working on at the moment?' Finn asked and she was startled back to the here and now.

'What?'

'You're carrying sewing needles. I'm not a great mind, but it does tell me there's likely to be sewing attached. Or do you bring them on the off chance you need to darn socks?'

'No, I…'

'Make tapestries? On the plane? Do you have a current project and, if so, can I see?'

She stared up at him and then stared down at

her feet. And his feet. One of his boots was dripping mud.

Strangely, it made him seem closer. More human.

She didn't show people her work, so why did she have a sudden urge to say...?

'Okay.'

'Okay?' he said cautiously.

'It's not pretty. And it's not finished. But if you'd really like to see...'

'Now?'

'When your foot's dry.'

'Why not with a wet foot?'

'My tapestry demands respect.'

He grinned. 'There speaks the lady of the castle.'

'I'm not,' she said. 'But my tapestry's up there with anything the women of this castle have done.' She smiled then, one of her rare smiles that lit her face, that made her seem...

Intriguing? No, he was already intrigued, he conceded.

Desirable?

Definitely.

'Are you sure?' she asked and he caught himself. He'd known this woman for how long?

'I'm very sure,' he told her. 'And, lady of the castle or not, your tapestry's not the only thing to deserve respect. I will take my boot off for you.'

'Gee, thanks,' she told him. 'Fifteen minutes. My bedroom. See you there.'

And she took off, running across the forecourt like a kid without a trouble in the world. She looked…free.

She looked beautiful.

Fifteen minutes with his boot off. A man had to get moving.

The tapestry was rolled and wrapped in the base of her kitbag. He watched as she delved into what looked to be the most practical woman's pack he'd ever seen. There were no gorgeous gowns or frilly lingerie here—just bike gear and jeans and T-shirts and sweaters. He thought briefly of the lawyer and his invitation to dinner in Dublin and found himself smiling.

Jo glanced up. 'What?'

'Is this why you said no to our lawyer's invite? I can't see a single little black dress.'

'I don't have a use for 'em,' she said curtly.

'You know, there's a costume gallery here,' he said and she stared.

'A costume gallery?'

'A store of the very best of what the Conaills have worn for every grand event in their history. Someone in our past has decided that clothes need to be kept as well as paintings. I found the store-room last night. Full of mothballs and gold embroidery. So if you need to dress up...'

She stared at him for a long moment, as if she was almost tempted—and then she gave a rueful smile and shook her head and tugged out the roll. 'I can't see me going out to dinner with our lawyer in gold embroidery. Can you? But if you want to see this...' She tossed the roll on the bed and it started to uncurl on its own.

Fascinated, he leaned over and twitched the end so the whole thing unrolled onto the white coverlet.

And it was as much as he could do not to gasp.

This room could almost be a servant's room, it was so bare. It was painted white, with a faded white coverlet on the bed. There were two dingy paintings on the wall, not very good, scenes of the local mountains. They looked as if they'd been painted by a long ago Conaill, with visions of artistic ability not quite managed.

But there was nothing 'not quite managed' about the tapestry on the bed. Quite simply, it lit the room.

It was like nothing he'd ever seen before. It was colour upon colour upon colour.

It was fire.

Did it depict Australia's Outback? Maybe, he thought, but if so it must be an evocation of what that could be like. This was ochre-red country, wide skies and slashes of river. There were wind-bent eucalypts with flocks of white cockatoos screeching from tree to tree... There were so many details.

And yet not. At first he could only see what looked like burning: flames with colour streaking through, heat, dry. And then he looked closer and it coalesced into its separate parts without ever losing the sense of its whole.

The thing was big, covering half the small bed, and it wasn't finished. He could see bare patches with only vague pencil tracing on the canvas, but he knew instinctively that these pencil marks were ideas only, that they could change.

For this was no paint by numbers picture. This was…

Breathtaking.

'This should be over the mantel in the great hall,' he breathed and she glanced up at him, coloured and then bit her lip and shook her head.

'Nope.'

'What do you do with them?'

'Give them to people I like. You can have this if you want. You pulled me out of a bog.'

And once more she'd taken his breath away.

'You just…give them away?'

'What else would I do with them?'

He was still looking at the canvas, seeing new images every time he looked. There were depths and depths and depths. 'Keep them,' he said softly. 'Make them into an exhibition.'

'I don't keep stuff.'

He hauled his attention from the canvas and stared at her. 'Nothing?'

'Well, maybe my bike.'

'Where do you live?'

'Where I can rent a room with good light for sewing. And where my sound system doesn't cause a problem. I like my music loud.' She shrugged. 'So there's another thing I own—a great speaker system to plug into my phone. Oh, and toothbrushes and stuff.'

'I don't get it.' He thought suddenly of his childhood, of his mother weeping because she'd dropped a plate belonging to her own mother. There'd been tears for a ceramic thing. And yet... his focus was drawn again to the tapestry. That Jo could work so hard for this, put so much of herself in it and then give it away...

'You reckon I need a shrink because I don't own stuff?' she asked and he shook his head.

'No. Though I guess...'

'I did see someone once,' she interrupted. 'When I was fifteen. I was a bit...wild. I got sent to a home for troublesome adolescents and they gave me a few sessions with a psychoanalyst. She hauled out a memory of me at eight, being moved on from a foster home. There was a fire engine I played with. I'd been there a couple of years so I guess I thought it was mine. When I went to pack, my foster mum told me it was a foster kid toy and I couldn't take it. The shrink told me it was significant, but I don't need a fire engine now. I don't need anything.'

He cringed for her. She'd said it blithely, as if it was no big deal, but he knew the shrink was right. This woman was wounded. 'Jo, the money we're both inheriting will give you security,' he said gently. 'No one can take your fire engine now.'

'I'm over wanting fire engines.'

'Really?'

And she managed a smile at that. 'Well, if it was a truly excellent fire engine...'

'You'd consider?'

'I might,' she told him. 'Though I might have to get myself a Harley with a trailer to carry it. Do Harleys come with trailers? I can't see it. Meanwhile, is it lunchtime?'

He checked his watch. 'Past. Uh oh. We need to face Mrs O'Reilly. Jo, you've been more than generous. You don't have to face her.'

'I do,' she said bluntly. 'I don't run away. It's not my style.'

Mrs O'Reilly had made them lunch but Finn wasn't sure how she'd done it. Her swollen face said she'd been weeping for hours.

She placed shepherd's pie in front of them and stood back, tried to speak and failed.

'I can't...' she managed.

'Mrs O'Reilly, there's no need to say a thing.' Jo reached for the pie and ladled a generous helping onto her plate. 'Not when you've made me pie. But I do need dead horse.'

'Dead horse?' Finn demanded, bemused, and Jo shook her head in exasperation.

'Honestly, don't you guys know anything? First, dead horse is Australian for sauce and second, shepherd's pie without sauce is like serving fish without chips. Pie and sauce, fish and chips, roast beef with Yorkshire pud... What sort of legacy are you leaving for future generations if you don't know that?'

He grinned and Mrs O'Reilly sniffed and sniffed again and then beetled for the kitchen. She returned with four different sauce bottles.

Jo checked them out and discarded three with disgust.

'There's only one. Tomato sauce, pure, unadulterated. Anything else is a travesty. Thank you, Mrs O'Reilly, this is wonderful.'

'It's not,' the woman stammered. 'I was cruel to you.'

'I've done some research into my mother over

the years,' Jo said, concentrating on drawing wiggly lines of sauce across her pie. 'She doesn't seem like she was good to anyone. She wasn't even good to me and I was her daughter. I can only imagine what sort of demanding princess she was when she was living here. And Grandpa didn't leave you provided for after all those years of service from you and your husband. I'd have been mean to me if I were you too.'

'I made you sleep in a single bed!'

'Well, that is a crime.' She was chatting to Mrs O'Reilly as if she were talking of tomorrow's weather, Finn thought. The sauce arranged to her satisfaction, she tackled her pie with gusto.

Mrs O'Reilly was staring at her as if she'd just landed from another planet, and Finn was feeling pretty much the same.

'A single bed's fine by me,' she said between mouthfuls. 'As is this pie. Yum. Last night's burned beef, though…that needs compensation. Will you stay on while we're here? You could make us more. Or would you prefer to go? Finn and I can cope on our own. I hope the lawyer has explained what you do from now on is your own choice.'

'He has.' She grabbed her handkerchief and blew her nose with gusto. 'Of course…of course I'll stay while you need me but now…I can have my own house. My own home.'

'Excellent,' Jo told her. 'If that's what you want, then go for it.'

'I don't deserve it.'

'Hey, after so many years of service, one burned dinner shouldn't make a difference, and life's never about what we deserve. I'm just pleased Finn and I can administer a tiny bit of justice in a world that's usually pretty much unfair. Oh, and the calendars in the kitchen…you like cats?'

'I…yes.'

'Why don't you have one?'

'Your grandfather hated them.'

'I don't hate them. Do you hate them, Finn?'

'No.'

'There you go,' Jo said, beaming. 'Find yourself a kitten. Now, if you want. And don't buy a cottage where you can't keep one.'

She was amazing, Finn thought, staring at her in silence. This woman was…stunning.

But Jo had moved on. 'Go for it,' she said, ladling more pie onto her fork. 'But no more talking. This pie deserves all my attention.'

They finished their pie in silence, then polished off apple tart and coffee without saying another word.

There didn't seem any need to speak. Or maybe there was, but things were too enormous to be spoken of.

As Mrs O'Reilly bustled away with the dishes, Jo felt almost dismayed. Washing up last night with Finn had been a tiny piece of normality. Now there wasn't even washing up to fall back on.

'I guess we'd better get started,' Finn said at last.

'Doing what?'

'Sorting?'

'What do we need to sort?' She gazed around the ornate dining room, at the myriad ornaments, pictures, side tables, vases, stuff. 'I guess lots of stuff might go to museums. You might want to keep some. I don't need it.'

'It's your heritage.'

'Stuff isn't heritage. I might take photographs of the tapestries,' she conceded. 'Some of them are old enough to be in a museum too.'

'Show me,' he said and that was the next few minutes sorted. So she walked him through the baronial hall, seeing the history of the Conaills spread out before her.

'It seems a shame to break up the collection,' Finn said at last. He'd hardly spoken as they'd walked through.

'Like breaking up a family.' Jo shrugged. 'People do it all the time. If it's no use to you, move on.'

'You really don't care?'

She gazed around at the vast palette of family life spread before her. Her family? No. Her mother had been the means to her existence, nothing more, and her grandfather hadn't given a toss about her.

'I might have cared if this had been my family,' she told him. 'But the Conaills were the reason I couldn't have a family. It's hardly fair to expect me to honour them now.'

'Yet you'd love to restore the tapestries.'

'They're amazing.' She crossed to a picture of a family group. 'I've been figuring out time frames, and I think this could be the great-great-grandpa we share. Look at Great-Great-Grandma. She looks a tyrant.'

'You don't want to keep her?'

'Definitely not. How about you?' she asked. 'Are you into family memorabilia?'

'I have a house full of memorabilia. My parents threw nothing out. And my brothers live very modern lives. I can't see any of this stuff fitting into their homes. I'll ask them but I know what their answers will be. You really want nothing but the money?'

'I wanted something a long time ago,' she told him. They were standing side by side, looking at the picture of their mutual forebears. 'You have no idea how much I wanted. But now...it's too late. It even seems wrong taking the money. I'm not part of this family.'

'Hey, we are sort of cousins.' And, before she knew what he intended, he'd put an arm around her waist and gave her a gentle hug. 'I'm happy to own you.'

'I don't...' The feel of his arm was totally disconcerting. 'I don't think I want to be owned.' And this was a normal hug, she told herself. A cousinly hug. There was no call to haul herself back in fright. She forced herself to stand still.

'Not by this great-great-grandma,' he conceded. 'She looks a dragon.' But his arm was still around her waist, and it was hard to concentrate on what he was saying. It was really hard. 'But you need to belong somewhere. There's a tapestry somewhere with your future on it.'

'I'm sure there's not. Not if it has grandmas and grandpas and kids and dogs.' Enough. She tugged away because it had to be just a cousinly hug; she wasn't used to hugs and she didn't need it. She didn't! 'I'm not standing still long enough to be framed.'

'That's a shame,' he told her, and something in the timbre of his voice made her feel...odd. 'Because I suspect you're worth all this bunch put together.'

'That's kissing the Blarney Stone.'

He shrugged and smiled and when he smiled she wanted that hug back. Badly.

'I'm not one for saying what I don't mean, Jo Conaill,' he told her. 'You're an amazing woman.'

'D...don't,' she stammered. For some reason the

hug had left her discombobulated. 'We're here to sort this stuff. Let's start now.'

And then leave, she told herself. The way she was feeling... The way she was feeling was starting to scare her.

The size of the place, the mass of furnishings, the store of amazing clothing any museum would kill for—the entire history of the castle was mind-blowing. It was almost enough to make her forget how weird Finn's hug made her feel. But there was work to be done. Figuring out the scale of their inheritance would take days.

Underground there were cellars—old dungeons?—and storerooms. Upstairs were 'living' rooms, apartment-sized chambers filled with dust-sheeted furniture. Above them were the bedrooms and up a further flight of stairs were the servants' quarters, rooms sparsely furnished with an iron cot and dresser.

Over the next couple of days they moved slowly through the place, sorting what there was. Most things would go straight to the auction rooms—almost all of it—but, by mutual consent, they decided to catalogue the things that seemed important. Detailed cataloguing could be done later by the auctioneers but somehow it seemed wrong to sell everything without acknowledging its existence. So they moved from room to room, taking notes, and she put the memory of the hug aside.

Though she had to acknowledge that she was grateful for his company. If she'd had to face this alone...

This place seemed full of ghosts who'd never wanted her, she thought. The costume store on its own was enough to repel her. All these clothes, worn by people who would never have accepted her. She was illegitimate, despised, discarded. She had no place here, and Finn must feel the same. Regardless of his inherited title, he still must feel the poor relation.

And he'd never fit in one of these cots, she thought as they reached the servants' quarters. She couldn't help glancing up at him as he opened the door on a third identical bedroom. He was big. Very big.

'It'd have to be a bleak famine before I'd fit in that bed,' he declared. He glanced down at the rough map drawn for them by Mrs O'Reilly. 'Now the nursery.'

The room they entered next was huge, set up as a schoolroom as well as a nursery. The place was full of musty furniture, with desks and a blackboard, but schooling seemed to have been a secondary consideration.

There were toys everywhere, stuffed animals of every description, building blocks, doll's houses, spinning tops, dolls large and small, some as much as three feet high. All pointing to indulged childhoods.

And then there was the rocking horse.

It stood centre stage in the schoolroom, set on its own dais. It was as large as a miniature pony, crafted with care and, unlike most other things in the nursery, it was maintained in pristine condition.

It had a glossy black coat, made, surely, with real horse hide. Its saddle was embellished with gold and crimson, as were the bridle and stirrups. Its ears were flattened and its dark glass eyes stared out at the nursery as if to say, *Who Dares Ride Me?*

And all around the walls were photographs and paintings, depicting every child who'd ever sat on this horse, going back maybe two hundred years.

Jo stared at the horse and then started a round of the walls, looking at each child in turn. These were beautifully dressed children. Beautifully cared for. Even in the early photographs, where children were exhorted to be still and serious for the camera or the artist, she could see their excitement. These Conaills were the chosen few.

Jo's mother was the last to be displayed. Taken when she was about ten, she was dressed in pink frills and she was laughing up at the camera. Her face was suffused with pride. *See*, her laugh seemed to say. *This is where I belong.*

But after her…nothing.

'Suggestions as to what we should do with all this?' Finn said behind her, sounding cautious, as if he guessed the well of emotion surging within. 'Auction the lot of them?'

'Where are you?' she demanded in a voice that didn't sound her own.

'Where am I where?'

'In the pictures.'

'You know I don't belong here.'

'No, but your great-great-grandfather…'

'I'm thinking he might be this one,' Finn said,

pointing to a portrait of a little boy in smock and pantaloons and the same self-satisfied smirk.

'And his son's next to him. Where's your great-grandfather? My great-grandpa's brother?'

'He was a younger son,' Finn said. 'I guess he didn't get to ride the horse.'

'So he left and had kids who faced the potato famine instead,' Jo whispered. 'Can we burn it?'

'What, the horse?'

'It's nasty.'

Finn stood back and surveyed the horse. It was indeed...nasty. It looked glossy, black and arrogant. Its eyes were too small. It looked as if it was staring at them with disdain. The poor relations.

'I'm the Lord of Glenconaill,' Finn said mildly. 'I could ride this nag if I wanted.'

'You'd squash it.'

'Then you could take my photograph standing over a squashed stuffed horse. Sort of a last hurrah.'

She tried to smile but she was too angry. Too full of emotion.

'How can one family have four sets of Monopoly?' Finn asked, gazing at the stacks of board games. 'And an Irish family at that? And what were we doing selling Bond Street?'

'They,' she snapped. 'Not we. This is not us.'

'It was our great-great-grandpa.'

'Monopoly wasn't invented then. By the time it was, you were the poor relation.'

'That's right, so I was,' he said cheerfully. 'But you'd have thought they could have shared at least one set of Monopoly.'

'They didn't share. Not this family.' She fell silent, gazing around the room, taking in the piles of…stuff. 'All the time I was growing up,' she whispered. 'These toys were here. Unused. They were left to rot rather than shared. Of all the selfish…' She was shaking, she discovered. Anger that must have been suppressed for years seemed threatening to overwhelm her. 'I hate them,' she managed and she couldn't keep the loathing from her voice. 'I hate it all.'

'Even the dolls?' he asked, startled.

'All of it.'

'They'll sell.'

'I'd rather burn them.'

'What, even the horse?' he asked, startled.

'Everything,' she said and she couldn't keep

loathing from her voice. 'All these toys… All this sense of entitlement… Every child who's sat on this horse, who's played with these toys, has known their place in the world. But not me. Not us. Unless your family wants them, I'd burn the lot.'

'My brothers have all turned into successful businessmen. My nieces and nephews have toys coming out their ears,' Finn said, a smile starting behind his eyes. There was also a tinge of under-standing. 'So? A bonfire? Excellent. Let's do it. Help me carry the horse downstairs.'

She stared, shocked. He sounded as if her sug-gestion was totally reasonable. 'What, now?'

'Why not? What's the use of having a title like mine if I can't use some of the authority that comes with it? Back at my farm the cows won't so much as bow when I walk past. I need to learn to be lordly and this is a start.' He looked at the horse with dislike. 'I think that coat's been slicked with oils anyway. He'll go up like a firecracker.'

'How can we?'

'Never suggest a bonfire if you don't mean it,' he said. 'There's nothing we Lords of Glenconaill like more than a good burning.' He turned and stared around at the assortment of expensive toys designed for favoured children and he grimaced. 'Selling any one of these could have kept a family alive for a month during the famine. If there was a fire engine here I'd say save it but there's not. Our ancestors were clearly people with dubious taste. Off with their heads, I say. Let's do it.'

CHAPTER FIVE

THE NURSERY WAS on the top floor and the stair-way was narrow. The horse went first, manoeu-vred around the bends with Finn at the head and Jo at the tail. Once downstairs, Finn headed for the stables and came back with crumbling timber while Jo carted more toys.

While they carried the horse down she was still shaking with anger. Her anger carried her through the first few armfuls of assorted toys but as Finn finished creating the bonfire and started helping her carry toys she felt her anger start to dissipate.

He was just too cheerful.

'This teddy looks like he's been in a tug of war or six,' Finn told her, placing the teddy halfway up the pyre. 'It's well time for him to go up in flames.'

It was a scruffy bear, small, rubbed bare in spots, one arm missing. One ear was torn off and his grin was sort of lopsided.

She thought of unknown ancestors hugging this bear. Then she thought of her mother and hardened her heart. 'Yes,' she said shortly and Finn cast her a questioning glance but headed upstairs for another load.

She followed, carting down a giraffe, two decrepit sets of wooden railway tracks and a box of blocks.

The giraffe was lacking a bit of stuffing. He was lopsided.

He was sort of looking at her.

'It's like the French Revolution,' Finn told her, stacking them neatly on his ever-growing pyre. 'All the aristocracy off to the Guillotine. I can just imagine these guys saying, "Let them eat cake".'

But she couldn't. Not quite.

The horse was sitting right on top of the pile, still looking aristocratic and nasty. The teddy was just underneath him. It was an old teddy. No one would want that teddy.

She was vaguely aware of Mrs O'Reilly watching from the kitchen window. She looked bemused. She wasn't saying anything, though.

These toys were theirs now, to do with as they wanted, Jo thought with a sudden stab of clarity.

Hers and Finn's. They represented generations of favoured children, but now...were she and Finn the favoured two?

She glanced at Finn, looking for acknowledgement that he was feeling something like she was—anger, resentment, sadness.

Guilt?

All she saw was a guy revelling in the prospect of a truly excellent bonfire. He was doing guy stuff, fiddling with toys so they made a sweeping pyre, putting the most flammable stuff at the bottom, the horse balanced triumphantly at the top.

He was a guy having fun.

'Ready?' he asked and she realised he had matches poised.

'Yes,' she said in a small voice and Finn shook his head.

'You'll have to do better than that. You're the lady of the castle, remember. It's an autocratic "Off with their heads", or the peasants will sense weakness. Strength, My Lady.'

'Off with their heads,' she managed but it was pretty weak.

But still, she'd said it and Finn looked at her for

a long moment, then gave a decisive nod and bent and applied match to kindling.

It took a few moments for the wood to catch. Finn could have put a couple of the more flammable toys at the base, she thought. That would have made it go up faster. Instead he'd left a bare spot so the fire would have to be strongly alight before it reached its target.

The teddy would be one of the first things to catch, she thought. The teddy with the missing ear and no arm. And an eye that needed a stitch to make his smile less wonky.

She could…

No. These were favoured toys of favoured people. They'd belonged to people who'd rejected her. People who'd given her their name but nothing else. People who'd made sure she had nothing, and done it for their own selfish ends.

The teddy… One stitch…

The flames were licking upward.

The giraffe was propped beside the teddy. There was a bit of stuffing oozing out from his neck. She could…

She couldn't. The fire was lit. The thing was done.

'Jo?' Finn was suddenly beside her, his hand

on her shoulder, holding her with the faintest of pressure. 'Jo?'

She didn't reply. She didn't take her eyes from the fire.

'You're sure you want to do this?' he asked.

'It's lit.'

'I'm a man who's into insurance,' he said softly and she looked down and saw he was holding a hose.

A hose. To undo what she needed to do.

The teddy...

Even the evil horse...

She couldn't do it. Dammit, she couldn't. She choked back a stupid sob and grabbed for the hose. 'Okay, put it out.'

'You want the fire out?'

'I'll do it.'

'You'll wet the teddy,' he said reproachfully. 'He'll get hypothermia as well as scorched feet. Trust me, if there's one thing I'm good at it's putting out fires.'

And he screwed the nozzle and aimed the hose. The water came out with satisfactory force. The wood under the teddy hissed and sizzled. Flames turned to smoke and then steam.

The teddy was enveloped with smoke but, before she realised what he intended, Finn stomped forward in his heavy boots, aimed the hose downward to protect his feet, then reached up and gathered the unfortunate bear.

And the giraffe.

He played the water for a moment longer until he was sure that no spark remained, then twisted the nozzle to off and turned back to her.

He handed her the teddy.

'Yours,' he said. 'And I know I said I have too much stuff, but I'm thinking I might keep the giraffe. I'll call him Noddy.'

She tried to laugh but it came out sounding a bit too much like a sob. 'N... Noddy. Because... because of his neck?'

'He's lost his stuffing,' Finn said seriously. 'He can't do anything but nod. And Teddy's Loppy because he's lopsided. He looks like he's met the family dog. One side looks chewed.'

'It'd be the castle dog. Not a family dog.'

'Ah, but that's where you're wrong,' he said, softly now, his gaze not leaving her face. As if he knew the tumult of stupid emotions raging within her. 'These people rejected us for all sorts of reasons but somehow they still are family. Our family. Toe-rags most of them, but some will have been decent. Some will have been weak, or vain or silly, and some cruel and thoughtless, but they were who they were. This...' he waved to the heap of toys spared from the flames '...this is just detritus from their passing.'

'Like us.'

'We're not detritus. We're people who make decisions. We're people who've spared a nursery full of toys and now need to think what to do with them.' He looked doubtfully at his lopsided giraffe. 'You did say you could sew.'

'I...I did.'

'Then I'll ask you to fix him so he can sit in my toolshed and watch me do shed stuff. Maybe Loppy can sit on your handlebars and watch you ride.'

'That'd be silly.'

'Silly's better than haunted.'

She stared at the pile of ancient toys, and then she turned and looked up at the castle.

'It's not its fault.'

'It's not even the horse's,' Finn said gently. 'Though I bet he collaborated.'

'He'd probably sell for heaps.'

'He would. I didn't like to say but there's been one like him in the window of the antique shop in the village at home. He has a three hundred pound price tag.'

'Three hundred... You didn't think to mention that when I wanted to burn him?'

'I do like a good bonfire.'

She choked on a bubble of laughter, emotion dissipating, and then she stared at the horse again. Getting sensible. 'We could give him away. To a children's charity or something.'

'Or we could sell him to someone who likes arrogant horses and give the money instead,' Finn told her. 'Think how many bears we could donate with three hundred pounds. Kids need friends, not horses who only associate with the aristocracy.'

There was a long silence. Mrs O'Reilly had disappeared from her window, no doubt confused by the on-again off-again bonfire. The sun was warm on Jo's face. In the shelter of the ancient outbuildings there wasn't a breath of wind. The stone walls around her were bathed in sunshine, their grey walls softened by hundreds of years of wear, of being the birthplace of hundreds of

Conaills, of whom only a few had been born with the privilege of living here.

'I guess we can't burn the whole castle because of one arrogant grandfather and one ditzy mother,' she said at last, and Finn looked thoughtful. Almost regretful.

'We could but we'll need more kindling.'

She chuckled but it came close to being a sob. She was hugging the teddy. Stupidly. She didn't hug teddies. She didn't hug anything.

'I suppose we should get rational,' she managed. 'We could go through, figure what could make money, sell what we can.'

'And make a bonfire at the end?' he asked, still hopefully, and her bubble of laughter stayed. A guy with the prospect of a truly excellent bonfire...

'The sideboards in the main hall are riddled with woodworm,' she told him, striving for sense. 'Mrs O'Reilly told me. They'd burn well.'

'Now you're talking.'

She turned back to the pile of unburned toys and her laughter faded. 'You must think I'm stupid.'

'I'm thinking you're angry,' Finn told her. He

paused and then added, 'I'm thinking you have
cause.'

'I'm over it.'

'Can you ever be over not being wanted?'

'That's just the trouble,' she said, and she stared
up at the horse again because it was easier looking at a horse than looking at Finn. He seemed to
see inside her, this man, and to say it was disconcerting would be putting it mildly. 'I *was* wanted.
Three separate sets of foster parents wanted to
adopt me but the Conaills never let it happen. But
I'm a big girl now. I have myself together.'

'And you have Loppy.'

'I'll lose him. I always lose stuff.'

'You don't have to lose stuff. With the money
from here you can buy yourself a warehouse and
employ a storeman to catalogue every last teddy.'
He gestured to the pile. 'You can keep whatever
you want.'

'I don't know…what I want.'

'You have time to figure it out.'

'So what about you?' she demanded suddenly.
'What do you want? You're a lord now. If you
could…would you stay here?'

'As a lord...' He sounded startled. 'No! But if I had time with these sheep...'

'What would you do with them?' she asked curiously, and he shrugged and turned and looked out towards the distant hills.

'Someone, years ago, put thought and care into these guys' breeding. They're tough, but this flock's different to the sheep that run on the bogs. Their coats are finer. As well, their coats also seem repellent. You put your hand through a fleece and you'll find barely a burr.'

'Could you take some back to your farm? Interbreed?'

'Why would I do that? Our sheep are perfect for the conditions there. These are bred for different conditions. Different challenges.' And he gazed out over the land and she thought he looked...almost hungry.

'You'd like a challenge,' she ventured and he nodded.

'I guess. But this is huge. And Lord of Glenconaill...I'd be ridiculous. Have you seen what the previous lords wore in their portraits?'

She grinned. 'You could ditch the leggings.'

'And the wigs?'

'Hmm.' She looked up at his gorgeous thatch of dark brown hair, the sun making the copper glints more pronounced, and she appeared to consider. 'You realise not a single ancestor is showing coloured hair. They wore hats or wigs or waited until they'd turned a nice, dignified white.'

'So if I'm attached to my hair I'm doomed to peasantry.'

'I guess.'

'Then peasantry it is,' he said and he smiled and reached out and touched her copper curls. 'I don't mind. I kind of like the company.'

And then silence fell. It was a strange kind of silence, Jo thought. A different silence. As if questions were being asked and answered, and thought about and then asked again.

The last wisps of leftover smoke were wafting upwards into the warm spring sunshine. The castle loomed behind them, vast and brooding, as if a reminder that something immeasurable was connecting them. A shared legacy.

A bond.

This man was her sort-of cousin, Jo thought, but the idea was a vague distraction, unreal. This man was not her family. He was large and male and beautiful. Yet he felt…

He felt unlike any of the guys she'd ever dated. He felt familiar in a sense that didn't make sense.

He felt…terrifying. Jo Conaill was always in control. She'd never gone out with someone who'd shaken that control, but just standing beside him…

'It feels right,' Finn said and she gazed up at him in bewilderment.

'What feels right?'

'I have no idea. To stand here with you?'

'I'm leaving.'

'So am I. We have lives. It's just…for here, for now…it feels okay.' He paused but there was no need for him to continue. She felt it too. This sense of…home.

What was she thinking? Home wasn't here. Home wasn't this man.

'My home's my bike,' she said, out of nowhere, and she said it too sharply, but he nodded as if she'd said something that needed consideration.

'I can see that, though the bike's pretty draughty. And there's no bath for when you fall into bogs.'

'I don't normally fall into bogs.'

'I can see that too. You're very, very careful, despite that bad girl image.'

'I don't have a bad girl image.'

'Leathers and piercings?' He smiled down at her, a smile that robbed his words of all possible offence. And then he lifted her arm to reveal a bracelet tattoo, a ring of tiny rosebuds around her wrist. 'And tattoos. My nieces and nephews will think you're cool.'

'Your nieces and nephews won't get to see it.'

'You don't want to meet them?'

'Why would I want to?'

'They're family, too.'

'Not my family.'

'It seems to me,' he said softly, 'that family's where you find it. And it also seems that somehow you've found it. Your hair gives you away.'

'If we're talking about my red hair then half of Ireland has it.'

'It's a very specific red,' he told her. 'My daddy had your hair and I know if I've washed mine nicely you can see the glint of his colour in mine.' And he lifted a finger and twisted one of her short curls. His smile deepened, an all-enveloping smile that was enough to make a woman sink into it.

'Family,' he said softly. 'Welcome to it, Jo Conaill. You and your teddy.'

'I don't want...'

'Family? Are you sure?'

'Y...yes.'

'That's a big declaration. And a lonely one.' He turned so he was facing her, then tilted her chin a little so her gaze was meeting his. 'I might have been raised in poverty, but it seems to me that you've been raised with the more desperate need. Does no one love you, Jo Conaill?'

'No. I mean...' Why was he looking at her? Why was he smiling? It was twisting something inside her, and it was something she'd guarded for a very long time. Something she didn't want twisting.

'I won't hurt you, Jo,' he said into the stillness and his words made whatever it was twist still more. 'I promise you that. I would never hurt you. I'm just saying...'

And then he stopped...saying.

Finn Conaill had been trying to work it out in his head. Ever since he'd met her something was tugging him to her. Connecting.

It must be the family connection, he'd thought. Or it must be her past.

She looked stubborn, indecisive, defiant.

She looked afraid.

She'd taken a step back from him and she was staring down at the bear in her arms as if it was a bomb about to detonate.

She didn't want family. She didn't want home. And yet...

She wanted the teddy. He knew she did.

By now he had some insight into what her childhood must have been. A kid alone, passed from foster family to foster family. Moved on whenever the ties grew so strong someone wanted her.

Learning that love meant separation. Grief.

Learning that family wasn't for her.

A cluster of wild pigeons was fussing on the cobblestones near the stables. Their soft cooing was a soothing background, a reassurance that all was well on this peaceful morning. And yet all wasn't well with this woman before him. He watched her stare down at the teddy with something akin to despair.

She wanted the teddy. She wanted...more.

Only she couldn't want. Wanting had been battered out of her.

She was so alone.

Family... The word slammed into his mind and stayed. He'd been loyal to Maeve for so many years he couldn't remember and he'd thought that loyalty was inviolate. But he'd known Jo for only three days, and somehow she was slipping into his heart. He was starting to care.

'Jo...' he said into the silence and she stared up at him with eyes that were hopelessly confused, hopelessly lost.

'Jo,' he said again.

And what happened next seemed to happen of its own volition. It was no conscious movement on his part, or hers.

It was nothing to do with them and yet it was everything.

He took the teddy from her grasp and placed it carefully on the ground.

He took her hands in his. He drew her forward—and he kissed her.

Had he meant to?

He didn't have a clue. This was unchartered territory.

For this wasn't a kiss of passion. It wasn't a kiss he'd ever experienced before. In truth, in its beginning it hardly felt like a kiss.

He tilted her chin very gently, with the image of a wild creature strongly with him. She could pull away, and he half expected her to. But she stayed passive, staring mutely up at him before his mouth met hers. Her chin tilted with the pressure of his fingers and she gazed into his eyes with an expression he couldn't begin to understand. There was a sort of resigned indifference, an expression which should have had him stepping back, but behind the indifference he saw a flare of frightened...hope?

He didn't want her indifferent, and it would be worse to frighten her. But the hope was there, and she was beautiful and her mouth was lush and partly open. And her eyes invited him in...

It was the gentlest of kisses, a soft, tentative exploration, a kiss that understood there were boundaries and he wasn't sure where they were but he wasn't about to broach them.

His kiss said *Trust me*. His kiss matched that flare of hope he was sure he'd seen. His kiss said, *You're beautiful and I don't understand it but something inside is drawing me to you.* And it said, *This kiss is just the beginning.*

Her first reaction was almost hysterical. Her roller coaster of emotions had her feeling this was happening to someone other than her.

But it was her. She was letting the Lord of Glenconaill kiss her.

Was she out of her mind?

No. Of course she wasn't. This was just a kiss, after all, and she was no prude. She was twenty-eight years old and there'd been men before. Of course there had. Nothing serious—she didn't do serious—but she certainly had fun. And this man was lovely. Gorgeous even. She could take him right now, she thought. She could tug him to her bed, or maybe they should use his bed because hers was ridiculously small. And then she could tear off his gear and see his naked body, which she was sure would be excellent, and she was sure the sex would be great...

Instead of which, her lips were barely touching his and her body was responding with a fear that said, *Go no further.* Go no further because one thing she valued above all others was control, and if she let this man hold her...

Except he was holding her. His kiss was warm and strong and true.

True? What sort of description was that for a kiss?

But then, in an instant, she was no longer thinking of descriptions. She wasn't thinking of anything at all. The kiss was taking over. The kiss was taking her to places she'd never been before. The kiss was...mind-blowing.

It was as if there'd been some sort of shorting to her brain. Every single nerve ending was snapped to attention, discarding whatever it was they'd been concentrating on and rerouting to her mouth. To his mouth. To the fusing of their bodies.

To the heat of him, to the strength, to the feeling of solid, fierce desire. For this was no cousinly kiss. This wasn't even a standard kiss between man and woman or if it was it wasn't something Jo had ever experienced before.

She was losing her mind. No, she'd lost it. She was lost in his kiss, melting, moulding against him, opening her lips, savouring the heat, the taste, the want—and she wanted more.

Her body was screaming for more. That was what all those nerve endings were doing—they'd forgotten their no doubt normally sensible functions and they were screaming, *This is where you're meant to be. Have. Hold.*

This is your...your...

No.

Whatever it was, whatever her body had been about to yell, she was suddenly closing down in fright. She was tugging away, pushing, shoving back. He released her the instant she pushed. She stood in the silent courtyard and stared at him as if he had two heads.

He didn't have two heads. He was just a guy. Just a stranger who happened to be vaguely related.

He was just the guy who'd saved her teddy.

She stared down at the bear at her feet, gasped and stooped to grab it. But Finn was before her, stooping to pick it up before she did. Their gaze met on the way up, and he handed over the bear with all solemnity.

'Was that why we stopped?' he asked. 'Because you'd dropped your bear?'

'Don't...don't be ridiculous.'

'Then don't look scared. Sweetheart, it was just a kiss.'

'I'm not your sweetheart.'

'No.'

'And I couldn't care less about the teddy.' But she did, she realised.

Why?

Because Finn had offered to burn it for her?

Because Finn had saved it?

The stupid twisting inside her was still going on and she didn't understand it. She didn't want it. It felt as if she was exposing something that hurt.

'We can give these things to charity,' she managed. 'That'd be more sensible than burning.'

'Much more sensible,' he agreed. Then he picked up the giraffe. 'I'll still be keeping this lad, though. No one would be wanting a stuffed giraffe with a wobbly neck.'

'I'll mend him for you.'

'That would be a kindness. But he's still not going to charity. How about Loppy?'

'I guess...I'm keeping him as well.' She was still wary, still unsure what had just happened. Still scared it might happen again.

'Then here's a suggestion,' he said, and the cheerful ordinariness was back in his voice, as if the kiss had never happened. 'There's a trailer in the stables. I'll hook it up and cart these guys—with the exception of Loppy and Noddy—into the village before the night dew falls. That'll stop us needing to cart them upstairs again. Meanwhile, you do some mending or take a walk or just wander the parapets and practice being Lady of the Castle. Whatever you want. Take some space to get to know Loppy.'

'I...thank you.' It was what she needed, she conceded. Space.

'Take all the time you need,' Finn said and then his smile faded and the look he gave her was questioning and serious. 'We're here until the documents can be signed. We do need to figure if there's anything in this pile to keep. But Jo...'

'Y... Yes?'

'Never, ever look at me again as if you're afraid of me,' he told her. 'We can organise things another way. I can stay in the village, or you can if that makes you feel safer. Whatever you like. But I won't touch you and I won't have you scared of me.'

'I'm not.'

'Yes, you are,' he said gently. 'And it needs to stop now.'

* * *

It took a couple of hours to link the trailer, pack the toys and cart them into the village. In truth, it was wasted time—there was so much in the castle to be sorted and dispersed that taking one load to the local charity shop was a speck in the ocean.

But he knew Jo needed him to leave. He'd kissed her, he'd felt her respond, he'd felt the heat and the desire—and then he'd felt the terror.

He wasn't a man to push where he wasn't wanted. He wasn't a man who'd ever want a woman to fear him.

And then there was the complication of Maeve and her father's expectations. He was well over it. The whole thing made him feel tired, but Maeve had left loose ends that needed to be sorted and they needed to be sorted now.

He was almost back at the castle but somehow he didn't want to be taking the complication of Maeve back there. He pulled to the side of the road and rang.

'Finn.' Maeve's voice was flat, listless. Normally he'd be sympathetic, gently pushing her to tell him what was happening but today things felt more urgent.

'Have you told him?'

'I can't. I told you I can't. That's why I came to see you. Finn, he'll be so upset. He's wanted us to marry for so long. He's already had a heart attack. It'll kill him.'

'That's a risk you have to take. Keeping the truth from your father any longer is dumb.'

'Then come and tell him with me. You can placate him. He's always thought of you as his son.'

'But I'm not his son,' he said gently. 'Maeve, face it.'

'Give me another week. Just a few more days.'

'By the time I come home, Maeve.' His voice was implacable. 'It has to be over.'

There was a moment's pause. Then… 'Why? You've met someone else?' And, astonishingly, she sounded indignant.

And that was what he got for loyalty, he thought grimly. An ex-fiancée who still assumed he was hers.

'It's none of your business, Maeve,' he told her and somehow forced his voice back to gentleness. 'Whatever I do, it's nothing to do with you.'

He disconnected but he stayed sitting on the roadside for a long time.

Loyalty…

It sat deep with him. Bone-deep. It was the reason he couldn't have walked away from his mam and brothers when his dad died. It would have been far easier to get a job in Dublin, fending for himself instead of fighting to eke out an existence for all of them. But the farm was his home and he'd fought to make it what it was, supporting his family until the need was no longer there. And by then the farm felt a part of him.

And Maeve? Maeve was in the mix too. She'd been an only child, his next door neighbour, his friend. Her father dreamed of joining the two farms together, and Finn's loyalty to that dream had always been assumed.

Maeve had smashed that assumption. He should be sad, he thought, but he wasn't. Just tired. Tired of loyalty?

No.

He could see the castle in the distance, solid, vast, a piece of his heritage. A piece of his country's heritage. Could old loyalties change? Shift?

His world seemed out of kilter. He wasn't sure

how to right it but somehow it seemed to have a new centre.

A woman called Jo?

It was too soon, he told himself. It was far too soon, but for now…for now it was time to return to the castle.

Time to go…to a new home?

CHAPTER SIX

JO SEEMED TO spend the next three days avoiding him as much as she could. The tension between them was almost a physical thing. The air seemed to bristle as they passed, so they spent their time doing what their separate skills required, separately.

Finn took inventory of the farm, working his way through the flocks of sheep, looking at what needed to be done before any sale took place. Inside the castle, the personal stuff was deemed to be Jo's, to do with what she wanted. She, after all, was the granddaughter of the house, Finn said firmly. She wanted none of it—apart from one battered bear—but things needed to be sorted.

She had three categories.

The first contained documents that might be important and photographs she decided to scan and file electronically in case someone in the future—not her—needed to reference them.

The second was a list of the things that seemed to go with the castle—the massive furnishings, the tapestries, the portraits.

The third contained items to be sold or given to museums. That included the storeroom full of ancient clothes. At some point in the far distant past, one of their ancestors had decided the amazing clothes worn on ceremonial occasions by generations of Conaills were worth preserving. A storeroom had been made dry and mothproof. The clothes smelled musty and were faded with age but they were still amazing.

'A museum would kill for them,' Jo told Finn.

He'd come in to find her before dinner. She was on the storeroom floor with a great golden ball-gown splayed over her knees. The white under-skirt was yellowed with age, but the mass of gold embroidery worked from neckline to hem made it a dazzle of colour.

'Try it on,' Finn suggested and Jo cast him a look that was almost scared. That was what he did to her, he thought ruefully. One kiss and he had her terrified.

'I might damage it.'

'I will if you will,' he told her. He walked across

to a cape that would have done Lord Byron proud. 'Look at this. Are these things neckcloths? How do you tie them? I'd have to hit the Internet. I'm not sure of the boots, though—our ancestors' feet seems to have been stunted. But if I can find something... Come on, Jo. We're eating dinner in that great, grand dining room. Next week we'll be back to being Finn the Farmer and Jo the Barista. For tonight let's be Lord and Lady Conaill of Castle Glenconaill. Just for once. Just because we can.'

Just because we can. The words echoed. She looked up at him and he could see the longing. Tattoos and piercings aside, there was a girl inside this woman who truly wanted to try on this dress.

'Dare you,' he said and she managed a smile.

'Only if you wear tights.'

'Tights?'

'Leggings. Breeches. Those.' She pointed to a pair of impossibly tight pants.

'Are you kidding? I'll sing falsetto for ever.'

'Dare you,' she said and suddenly she was grinning and so was he and the thing was done.

He was wearing a magnificent powder-blue coat with gilt embroidery, open to just above his knees.

He'd somehow tied an intricate cravat, folds of soft white linen in some sort of cascade effect that was almost breathtaking. He looked straight out of the pages of the romance novel she'd read on the plane. His dark hair was neat, slicked, beautiful. And he was wearing breeches.

Or pantaloons? What were they called? It didn't matter. They clung to his calves and made him look breathtakingly debonair. He looked so sexy a girl's toes could curl.

She forced herself to look past the sexy legs, down to his shoes. They looked like slippers, stretched but just on. More gilt embroidery.

More beauty.

'If you're thinking my toes look squashed you should feel everything else,' he growled, following her gaze. 'How our ancestors ever fathered children is beyond me. But Jo...' He was staring at her in incredulity. 'You look...beautiful.'

Why that had the power to make her eyes mist she had no idea. He was talking about the clothes, she told herself. Not her.

'You're beautiful already,' he told her, making a lie of her thoughts. 'But that dress...'

She was wearing the dress he'd seen on her

knee and why wouldn't she? This was a Cinderella dress, pure fantasy, a dress some long ago
Conaill maiden had worn to a ball and driven
suitors crazy. She'd have to have had warts all
over her not to drive suitors crazy, Jo thought.
This dress was a work of art, every inch embellished, golden and wondrous. It was almost more
wondrous because of the air of age and fragility
about it.

But it fitted her like a glove. She'd tugged it on
and it had slipped on her like a second skin. The
boned bodice pushed her breasts up, cupping them
so their swell was accentuated. She'd powdered
her curls. She'd found a tiara in her grandfather's
safe, and a necklace that surely wasn't diamonds
but probably was. There were earrings to match.

She, too, was wearing embroidered dancing slippers. She needed a ball, she thought, and then she
thought, no, she had enough. She had her beautiful gown.

She had her Prince Charming.

And oh, those breeches…

'Our ancestors would be proud of us,' Finn told
her and offered his arm, as befitted the Lord of
the Castle offering his arm to his Lady as they

approached the staircase to descend to the dining hall.

She hesitated only for a moment. This was a play, she told herself. It wasn't real.

This was a moment she could never forget. She needed to relax and soak it in.

She took his arm.

'Our ancestors couldn't possibly not be proud of us,' she told him as they stepped gingerly down the stairs in their too-tight footwear. But it wasn't her slippers making her feel unsafe, she thought. It was Finn. He was so big. He was so close.

He was so gorgeous.

'Which reminds me…' He sounded prosaic, but she suspected it was an effort to make himself sound prosaic. She surely couldn't. 'What are we going to do with our ancestors?'

'What do you mean?'

'All the guys who wore these clothes. All the pictures in the gallery.'

'I guess…they'll sell with the castle. They can be someone else's ancestors.'

'Like in Gilbert and Sullivan? Do you know *The Pirates of Penzance*?' He twirled an imaginary moustache and lowered his voice to that of a raspy English aristocrat. 'Major General Stanley, at your service,' he said, striding ahead down the staircase and turning to face up to her. Prince Charming transformed yet again. 'So, My Lady,' he growled up at her. 'In this castle are ancestors, but we're about to sell the castle and its contents. So we don't know whose ancestors they will be. Mind, I shudder to think that an unknown buyer could bring disgrace upon what, I have no doubt, is an unstained escutcheon. Our escutcheon. We'll have to be very careful who we sell it to.'

'Escutcheon?' she said faintly and he grinned.

'Our unblemished pedigree, marred only by you not appearing to have a daddy, and me being raised surrounded by pigs. But look at us now.' He waved down at the grand entrance and the two astonishing suits of armour. 'Grand as anything. Forget Major General Stanley. I'm dressed as Lord Byron but I believe I aspire to the Pirate King. All I need is some rigging to scale and some minions to clap in irons.'

'I vote not to be a minion.'

'You can be my pirate wench if you like,' he said kindly. 'To scrub decks and the like.'

'In this dress?'

He grinned. 'You could pop into a bucket and then swish across the decks with your wet dress. The decks would come up shiny as anything.' And then he paused and smiled at her, a smile that encompassed all of her. Her beautiful dress with its neckline that was a bit too low and accentuated her breasts. Her powdered curls. Her diamond necklace and earrings and tiara.

But somehow his smile said he saw deeper. His smile made her blush before he said anything more.

'Though I'd have better things to do with my wench than have her scrubbing decks,' he said— and he leered.

How could she blush when there was a bubble of laughter inside? And how could she blush when he was as beautiful as she was?

And suddenly she wanted to play this whole game out to its natural conclusion. She wanted to play Lady to his Lord. She wanted Finn to sweep her up in her beautiful ballgown and carry her upstairs and…

And nothing! She had to be sensible. So somehow she lifted her skirts, brushed past him and hiked down the remaining stairs and across the hall. She removed her tiara and put it safely aside, lifted the helmet from one of the suits of armour and put it on her head. Then she grabbed a sword and pointed it.

'Want to try?' she demanded. 'This wench knows how to defend herself. Come one step closer...'

'Not fair. I don't have my cutlass.' He glanced ruefully at his side. 'I think there's a ceremonial sword to go with this but I left it off.'

'Excellent.' Her voice was sounding a bit muffled.

'Jo?'

'Yep.'

'Can you see in that thing?'

'Nope.'

'So if I were to come closer...'

'I might whirl and chop. Or...'

'Or?'

Or...uh oh... She bent—with difficulty—boned bodices weren't all that comfortable—and laid the sword carefully on the floor. She raised her hands to the helmet. 'Or you might help me off with this,' she said, a bit shakily. 'It sort of just slid on. Now...it seems to be heavy.'

'A Lady of the Castle pretending to be a pirate wench, in a suit of armour?' He stood back and chuckled. 'I think I like it.'

What was she doing, asking this man for help? What a wuss! She bent to retrieve her sword, an action only marred by having to grope around her swirling skirts. With it once more in her hand, she pointed it in what she hoped was his general direction. 'Help me or the giraffe gets it,' she muttered.

'Noddy?' he demanded, astounded. 'What's Noddy done to you?'

'Nothing, but we knights don't skewer lords. We hold them to ransom and skewer their minions instead.'

'So how will you find my...minion? Noddy's up in my bedroom.' He was smiling at her. It was a bit hard to see through the visor but she knew he was smiling.

'With difficulty,' she conceded. 'But I stand on my principles.' She tried again to tug her helmet off and wobbled in her tight slippers but she held onto her defiance. 'If you're the pirate king, I insist on equal status.'

'We can go back to being Lord and Lady of our real life castle.'

'I guess.' She sighed. Enough. She had to confess. 'Finn, this may look like a bike helmet but it seems the helmet manufacturers of days of yore had a lot to learn. Help me get this off!'

He chuckled. 'Only if you guarantee that Noddy's safe.'

'Noddy's safe.'

'And no ransom?'

'Not if I don't have to play wench.'

'Are you in a position to negotiate?'

'I believe,' she said, 'that I still have a sword and I stand between you and your dinner.'

'That's playing mean.'

'Help me off with the helmet or we'll both starve,' she said and he chuckled again and came forward and took the sword from her hands and gently raised her helmet.

She emerged, flushed and flustered, and it didn't help that he was only inches away from her face and he was smiling down at her. And he did look like the Lord of His Castle. And her skirts were rustling around her and his dangerous eyes were laughing, and how they did that she didn't know but it was really unfair. And the look of him... The feel of his coat... The brush of his fingers...

The odds were so stacked in this man's favour. He was Lord to her Lady.

Only, of course, he wasn't. He wasn't hers. He wasn't anyone's and she didn't want anyone anyway. In less than a week this fantasy would be over. She'd be on the road again, heading back to Australia, and she'd never see him again and that was what she wanted, wasn't it?

Goodbyes. She was really good at them.

Goodbyes were all she knew.

'Jo?'

She must have been looking up at him for too long. The laughter had faded, replaced by a troubled look.

'I...thank you.' She snatched the helmet from his hands and jammed it back on its matching body armour. Which should have meant she had her back to him, but he took the sword and came to stand beside her, putting the sword carefully back into a chain-meshed hand.

He was too close. She was too flustered. He was too...

'Dinner! And don't you both look beautiful!' Mrs O'Reilly's voice was like a boom behind them. How long had she been standing there? Had

Finn known she was standing there? Okay, now it was time for her colour to rise. She felt like grabbing the sword again and...

'Knives and forks at noon?' Finn said and the laughter was back in his voice. He took her hand and swung her to face the housekeeper, for all the world like a naughty child holding his accomplice fast for support. 'Are we late, Mrs O'Reilly?'

'I'll have you know those clothes haven't been touched for hundreds of years. And, as for that armour, it's never been moved.'

'See,' Finn told Jo mournfully. 'I told you we're more interested in finance than war. Ours is not a noble heritage.'

'Just as well we're selling it then.'

'Indeed,' he said but his voice didn't quite sound right. She flashed him a questioning glance but he had himself together again fast. 'We're sorry, Mrs O'Reilly. It's to be hoped nothing's come to any grief.'

'It does suit you both,' the housekeeper admitted. 'Eh, you look lovely. And it's yours to do with what you want.'

'Just for a week,' Finn told her. 'Then it's every ancestor for himself. Off to the highest bidder.

Meanwhile, Lady of the Castle Glenconaill, let's forget about war. Let's eat.'

'Yes, My Lord,' she said meekly, but things had changed again and she didn't know how.

After that they went back to their individual sorting but somehow the ridiculous banter and the formal dinner in the beautiful clothes had changed things. A night dressed up as Lord and Lady had made things seem different. Lighter? Yes, but also somehow full of possibilities. Finn didn't understand how but that was the way his head was working.

Through the next couple of days they reverted to practicalities. Jo still worked inside. He drafted the sheep into age and sex, trying to assess what he had. He brought the two cows up to the home field. One was heavy with calf and looked badly malnourished.

'They're not ours,' Mrs O'Reilly told him when he questioned her at breakfast. 'They were out on the road a couple of weeks back and a passing motorist herded them through the gate. Then he came here and harangued us for letting stock roam. I let them stay. I didn't know what else to do.'

'You've been making all the decisions since my grandfather became ill?' Jo demanded.

'I have.'

'Then I think we need to increase Mrs O'Reilly's share of the estate,' she declared.

'There's no need to do that,' the housekeeper said, embarrassed. 'There's nothing else I need.' She paused mid-clearing and looked around the massive dining room with fondness. Finn's suggestion that they eat in the kitchen had been met with horror so they'd decided for a week they could handle the splendour. 'Though I would like more time here. Do you think a new owner might hire me?'

'In a heartbeat,' Jo said soundly and the woman chuckled.

'Get on with you. But, if it happens, it'd be lovely.' She heaved a sigh and left and Finn turned impulsively to Jo.

'Come with me this morning.'

'What? Why?'

'Because I want you to?' There was little time left, he thought. Tomorrow the lawyer was due to return. They could sign the papers, and Jo could leave. He'd need to sort someone to take care of the livestock but Jo didn't need to stay for that. So the day after tomorrow—or even tomorrow night—Jo could be on her way back to Australia.

'I've found a bouncy bog,' he told her.

'A bouncy bog…?'

'Our south boundary borders the start of bog country. I checked it out yesterday. There's a patch that quakes like a champion.'

'You mean it sucks things down like it nearly sucked me?'

'I jumped,' he told her. 'And I lived to tell the tale. And Jo, I did it for you. The Lady of Castle Glenconaill would like this bog, I told myself, so here I am, my Lady, presenting an option. Sorting more paperwork or bog jumping.'

'There is…'

'More paperwork,' he finished for her. 'Indeed there is. I looked at what you've done last night and I'm thinking you've done a grand job. But surely the important stuff's sorted and maybe you could grant yourself one morning's holiday. No?'

She should say no.

Why?

Because she didn't trust him?

But she did trust him and that was the whole

problem, she decided. He was so darned trustworthy. And his smile was so lovely. And he was so…

Tempting.

Go and jump on a bog with Finn Conaill?

Go with Finn Conaill?

This guy might look like a farmer but she had to keep reminding herself who he was.

He was Lord Conaill of Castle Glenconaill.

And worse. He'd become…her friend?

And he'd kissed her and maybe that was the crux of the problem. He'd kissed her very thoroughly indeed and, even though he'd drawn away when she wanted and there'd been no mention of the kiss ever since, it was still between them. It sort of hovered…

And he'd worn breeches. And he'd looked every inch the Lord of Glenconaill.

And she was going home tomorrow! Or the next day if the lawyer was late. What harm could a little bog jumping do?

With a friend.

With Finn.

There was no harm at all, she told herself, so why were alarm bells going off right, left and centre?

'I don't think…' she started and he grinned.

'Chicken.'

'I'd rather be a chicken than a dead hen.'

'Do they say that in Australian schoolyards as well?' He was still smiling. Teasing.

'For good reason.'

'Bogs don't swallow chickens. Or not unless they're very fat. I'll hold you up, Jo Conaill. Trust me.'

And what was it that said a man who looked totally trustworthy—who *felt* totally trustworthy, for her body was still remembering how solid, how warm, *how much a woman*, this man made her feel—what was it that made her fear such a man assuring her he could be trusted?

What made her think she should run?

But he was still smiling at her, and his smile was no longer teasing but gentle and questioning, and it was as if he understood how fearful she was.

It was stupid not to go with him, she thought. She had one day left. What harm could a day make?

'All right,' she said ungraciously, and the laughter flashed back.

'What, no curtsy and "Thank You, Your Lord-ship, your kind invitation is accepted"?'

'Go jump,' she said crossly and he held out his hand.

'I will,' he said. 'Both of us will. Come and jump with me.'

For the last couple of days the amount of sorting had meant every time they came together there was so much to discuss there was little time for the personal. But now suddenly there wasn't. Or maybe there was but suddenly it didn't seem im-portant.

Jo was no longer sure what was important.

She'd never felt so at ease with anyone, she thought as they walked together over fields that grew increasingly rough the nearer they were to the estate boundaries. But right now that very ease was creating a tension all by itself.

She didn't understand it and it scared her.

She needed to watch her feet now. This was peat country and the ground was criss-crossed with scores of furrows where long lines of peat had been dug. That was what she needed to do before she went home, she thought. Light a peat fire. Tonight? Her last night?

The thought was enough to distract her. She slipped and Finn's hand was suddenly under her elbow, holding her steady.

She should pull away.

She didn't.

And then they were at a line of rough stone fencing. Finn stepped to the top stone and turned to help her.

As if she'd let him. She didn't need him.

She stepped up and he should have got out of the way, gone over the top, but instead he waited for her to join him.

There was only a tiny section of flat stone. She had no choice but to join him.

His arm came round and held her, whether she willed it or not, and he turned her to face the way they'd come.

'Look at the view from here.'

She did and it was awesome. The castle was built on a rise of undulating country, a vast monolith of stone. It seemed almost an extension of the country around it, rough hewn, rugged, truly impressive.

'For now, it's ours,' Finn said softly and Jo looked over the countryside, at the castle she'd heard about since childhood and never seen, and she felt...

Wrong.

Wrong that she should be signing a paper that said sell it to the highest bidder.

Wrong that she should be leaving.

But then she always left, she thought. Of course she did. What was new?

She tugged away from Finn, suddenly inexplicably angry. He let her go, but gently so she didn't wrench back but had time to find the footholds to descend to the other side.

To where the bog started.

'Beware,' Finn told her as she headed away from the wall, and she looked around her and thought, *Beware is right.*

It was the same sort of country she'd been caught in when Finn first found her. This wall wasn't just a property boundary then. It was the start of where the country turned treacherous.

For here were the lowlands. The grasses were brilliant green, dotted with tiny wildflowers. There were rivulets of clear water, like rivers in miniature. The ground swept away to the mountains beyond, interrupted only by the occasional wash of sleet-coloured water.

There were no birds. There seemed no life at all.

'I've been out on it,' Finn told her. 'It's safe. Come on; this is fun.'

And he took her hand.

Her first impulse was to tug away. Of course it was. Since when did she let anyone lead her anywhere? But this was Finn. This was Ireland. This was...right?

'I'm not hauling you anywhere you don't want to go,' Finn told her. 'This is pure pleasure.'

So somehow she relaxed, or sort of relaxed, as he led her across the stone-strewn ground to where the ground ceased being solid and the bog began. But his steps were sure. All she had to do was step where he stepped. And leave her hand in his.

Small ask.

'It doesn't hurt,' he said softly into the stillness.

'What doesn't hurt?'

'Trusting.'

She didn't reply. She couldn't. Her hand was in his, enveloped in his strength and surety.

Trust...

'That first day when I picked you up,' he said softly. 'I pretty near gave you a heart attack. I pretty near gave *me* a heart attack. You want to tell me what that was about?'

'No.'

'Okay,' he said lightly and led her a bit further. She was concentrating on her feet. Or she should be concentrating on her feet.

She was pretty much aware of his hand.

She was still pretty much aware of his question.

'I couldn't handle it,' she told him. 'I had a temper.'

'I guessed that,' he said and smiled. But he wasn't looking at her. He was concentrating on the ground, making sure each step he took was steady, and small enough so she could follow in his footsteps. It was the strangest sensation... 'So what couldn't you handle?'

'Leaving.'

'Mmm.' The silence intensified. There were frogs, she thought. There'd been frogs in the last bit of bog but there were more here. So it wasn't silent.

Except it was.

'Will you tell me?' he asked conversationally, as if it didn't matter whether she did or not, and then he went back to leading her across the bog.

If he left her now, she thought... If he abandoned her out here...

He wouldn't. But, even if he did, it wasn't a drama. He was stepping from stone to stone and she understood it now. If he left she wouldn't be in trouble.

She could leave. She could just turn around and go.

Will you tell me?

'I got attached,' she said softly, as if she didn't want to disturb the frogs, which, come to think of it, she didn't. 'Everywhere I went. I think... because my mother was overseas, because she didn't want anything to do with me, because no one knew who my father was, it was assumed I'd eventually be up for adoption. So I was put with people who were encouraged to love me. To form ties. And of course I grew ties back.'

'That sucks.'

'It was only bad when it was time to leave.'

'But when it was...'

'It was always after a full-on emotional commitment,' she told him. 'I'd stay for a couple of years and we'd get close. My foster parents would apply for adoption, there'd be ages before an answer came but when it did it was always the same. My mother didn't want me adopted. She'd say she was currently negotiating taking me herself so she'd like me transferred close to Sydney, Melbourne, Brisbane—always the city that was furthest from my foster parents. She said it was so she could fly in quickly from Ireland to pick me up. I got stoic in the end but I remember when I was little, being picked up and carried to the car, and everyone I loved was behind me and my foster mum was crying…I'm sorry, but the day you first saw me I'd been stuck in the bog for an hour and I was tired and jet-lagged and frightened and you copped a flashback of epic proportions. I'm ashamed of myself.'

Silence.

He felt his free hand ball into a fist. Anger surged, an anger so great it threatened to overwhelm him.

'Let's revisit our bonfire idea,' he said. 'I'd kind of like to burn the whole castle.' He was struggling to make his voice light.

'We've been there. I couldn't even burn the horse.'

'Mrs O'Reilly said it made three hundred and fifty pounds for the local charity shop,' he told her. 'For kids with cancer.'

'As long as the kids with cancer don't have to look into its sneering face.'

'But that's what you're doing,' he said gently. 'Coming back to Ireland. You're looking at a nursery full of toys owned by kids who were wanted. You're looking into its sneering face.'

'I don't want to burn it, though,' she said. She turned and gazed back across the boundary, back to the distant castle. 'It's people who are cruel, not things. And things can be beautiful. This is beautiful and the people are gone.'

'And so's the horse,' he said encouragingly. 'And we can go put thistles on Fiona's grave if you want.'

'That'd be childish. I'm over her.'

'Really?'

'As long as you don't pick me up.'

'I won't pick you up. But, speaking of childish... You don't want childish?'

'I...'

'Because what I've found here is really, really childish.' He took her hand again and led her a little way further to the base of a small rise. The grassland here looked lush and rich, beautifully green, an untouched swathe.

'Try,' he said, and let go her hand and gave her a gentle push. 'Jump.'

'What—me? Are you kidding? I'll be down to my waist again.'

'You won't. I've tried it.'

She stared at it in suspicion. 'The grass isn't squashed.'

'And there's no great holes where I sank. There's a whole ribbon of this, land that quakes beautifully but doesn't give. Trust me, Jo. Jump.'

Trust him. A man who wore leggings and intricate neckties and looked so sexy a girl could swoon. The Lord of Glenconaill Castle.

A man in work trousers and rolled-up sleeves.

A man who smiled at her.

She stared back at him, and then looked at the grassy verge. It looked beautiful.

The sun was shining on her face. The sound of a thousand frogs was a gentle choir across the bog.

Trust me.

She took a tentative step forward and put her weight on the grass.

The ground under her sagged and she leaped back. 'I don't think...'

'You're not sinking into mud. This is a much thicker thatch of grass than where you got stuck. I've tried it out. Look.' And he jumped.

The ground sagged and rose again. Jo was standing two or three feet away from him. The grasses quivered all the way across to her and she rode a mini wave.

She squealed in surprise, then stared down in astonishment. 'Really?'

He jumped again, grinning. 'I found it just for you. Try it.'

She jumped, just a little.

'Higher.'

'It'll...'

'It won't do anything. I told you before; I've tried it. I was here yesterday, scouting a good bit of bog to show you.'

'You did that...for me?'

'I can't have you going back to Australia thinking all Irish bogs are out to eat Australians.' He reached out and caught her hands. 'Bounce.'

'I...'

'Trust me. Bounce.'

Trust him. She looked up at him and he was smiling, and he was holding her hands and the warmth of him...the strength of him...

He wouldn't let her down. How did she know it? She just knew it.

'Bounce,' he said again, encouragingly, and she met his gaze and his smile said *Smile back* and somehow she felt herself relax.

She bounced and the lovely squishy grasses bounced with her and, to her amazement, she felt Finn do a smaller bounce as the quaking ground moved under him as well.

'It's like a water bed,' she breathed.

'I've never tried a water bed,' Finn admitted. 'I always thought they'd be weird.'

'But fun.'

'You've slept in one?'

'One of my foster mums had one. She had three foster kids and we all bounced. She was out one day and we bounced too much and she came home to floods. She wasn't best pleased.'

'I'd imagine,' Finn said, chuckling, and jumping himself so Jo bounced with him. 'Gruel and stale bread for a week?'

'Mops at twenty paces.' She bounced again, starting to enjoy herself. 'Foster parents are awesome.'

'Until you have to leave.'

'Let's not go there.' She bounced again, really high. The ground sagged but bounced back, so she and Finn were rocking with each other. The sun was on their faces. A couple of dozy sheep were staring over the stone wall with vague astonishment. A bird—a kestrel?—was cruising high in the thermals above them, maybe frog-hunting?

'I hope we're not squashing frogs,' she worried out loud and he grinned.

'Any self-respecting frog will be long gone. That was some squeal.'

'I don't squeal.'

'You did.'

'I might have,' she conceded, jumping again just because she could, just because it felt good, just because this man was holding her hands and for now it felt right. She felt right. She felt...as if this was her place. As if she had every right in the world to be here. As if this was her home? 'I had…provocation,' she managed. She was trying to haul her thoughts back to whether or not she'd squealed, but her thoughts were heading off on a tangent all of their own.

A tangent that was all about how this man was holding her and how good it felt and how wonderful that when she jumped he jumped, and when he jumped she jumped. And suddenly it had nothing to do with the bog they were jumping on but everything to do with how wonderful it was. With how wonderful *he* was.

'I should warn you, you're seeing the bog at its best,' Finn told her. 'Tomorrow it'll be raining. In fact this afternoon it may be raining. Or in half an hour. This is Ireland, after all.'

'I like Ireland.'

'You've seen approximately nought point one per cent of Ireland.'

'Then I like nought point one per cent. I like this part.'

'Me, too,' he said and jumped again and suddenly they were grinning at each other like idiots and jumping in sync and the world felt amazing. The world felt right.

'You want to explore a bit further?' he asked and

her hands were in his and suddenly she thought no matter where he wanted to take her she'd follow. Which was a stupid thought. She didn't do trust. She didn't...love?

There was a blinding thought, a thought so out of left field that she tugged her hands back and stared at him in confusion. She'd known this guy for just over a week. You couldn't make decisions like that in a week.

Could you?

'What's wrong?' he asked gently and she stared at him and somehow the confusion settled.

He wasn't asking her to love him. He was asking her to explore the landscape.

With him.

'You know I won't let you sink,' he told her and she looked up at him and made a decision. A decision based on his smile. A decision based on the gentleness of his voice.

A decision not based one little bit on how good-looking he was, or how big, or how the sun glinted on his dark hair or how the strength of him seemed like an aura. He was a farmer born and bred. He was a farmer who was now the Lord of Glenconaill. Who could transform at will...

No. The decision wasn't based on that at all. It was simply that she wanted to see more of this amazing country before she left.

'Yes, please,' she said and then, because it was only sensible and Jo Conaill prided herself on being sensible, she slipped her hands back into his. After all, he was her guarantee...not to sink.

'Yes, please,' she said again. 'Show me all.'

He wished he knew more about this country.

If you drove quickly across bog country you could easily take it for a barren waste. But if you walked it, as he and Jo were walking it, taking care to stick to ground he knew was solid but venturing far from the roads, where the ground rose and fell, where the streams trickled above and below ground, where so many different plants eked out a fragile life in this tough terrain...if you did that then you realised the land had a beauty all its own. He knew the artist in Jo was seeing it as it should be seen.

And she was asking questions. She'd tighten her hold on his hand and then stoop, forcing him to stoop with her. 'What's this?' she'd ask, fingering some tiny, delicate flower, and he didn't know what it was and he could have kicked himself for not knowing.

He knew what grew on his farm. He didn't know this place.

But it was fascinating and Jo's enjoyment made it more so.

'I need to sketch,' she whispered, gazing around her with awe. 'I never knew...'

But she was going home, he thought, and more and more the thought was like grey fog.

They'd had their week at the castle. They'd had their fairy tale. After tomorrow they'd go back to their own lives. The castle would be nothing more than an eye-watering amount in their bank accounts.

And, as if on cue, the sun went under a cloud. He glanced up and saw the beginnings of storm clouds. You didn't expect anything else in this country. The land was so wet that as soon as it was warm, condensation formed clouds and rain followed.

It was kind of comforting. A man knew where he was with this weather—and if he had to feel grey then why not let it rain?

'We need to get back,' he told her. 'It'll be raining within the hour.'

'Really?'

'Really.'

She paused and gazed around her, as if drinking in the last view of this amazing landscape. Her hand was still in his.

Her hand felt okay. It felt good.

The feeling of grey intensified. Tomorrow it'd be over. He'd be back on his farm, looking towards the future.

He'd be rich enough to expand his farm to something enormous. He could do whatever he liked.

Why didn't that feel good?

'Okay,' Jo said and sighed. 'Time to go.'

And it was.

CHAPTER SEVEN

EXCEPT THERE WAS the cow.

They reached the home field behind the castle just as the first fat raindrops started to fall. Jo's hand was still in his—why let it go? Finn helped her climb the last stile and then paused.

He'd brought the two stray cows into the paddock nearest the stables so he could give them extra feed and watch the younger cow who he thought was close to calving. She was very young, he'd decided as he'd brought her to the top field, barely more than a calf herself. The cow she was with was probably her mother.

And now she was definitely calving, heaving with futile effort. The older cow was standing back, watching, backing off a little and then edging nearer, as if not knowing what was happening but frightened regardless.

She had reason to be frightened, Finn acknowledged as he got a clear look at what was going on.

The ground around the little cow was flattened, as if she'd been down for a while. Her eyes were wild and rolling back.

Damn.

'Calving?' Jo asked and Finn nodded grimly. He approached with caution, not wanting to scare her more than she already was, but the little cow was too far gone to be scared of anything but what was happening to her body.

'Lord Conaill?'

Mrs O'Reilly was standing on the castle side of the field's stone wall underneath a vast umbrella. 'Thank heaven you've come. She's been down for two hours and nothing's happening. I didn't know where you were so I telephoned the veterinary. He's away. The lad who answers his calls says there's nothing he can do. If it's a stray cow, the kindest thing would be to shoot her, he said, so I took the liberty of unlocking your grandfather's gun cabinet. Which one would you be wanting to use?'

She was holding up guns. Three guns!

This was a stray cow, with no known lineage. It was a straggly, half starved animal and its mother looked little better. She'd fetch little at market, maybe a small amount for pet food.

He glanced back at Jo. Her face was expressionless.

'I've used the shotgun on the sheep when I had to,' Mrs O'Reilly said, sounding doubtful. 'But it made a dreadful mess. Would you be knowing more about them?'

Finn had been stooping over the cow. Now he straightened and stared at her. 'You shot...'

'Two sheep,' she told him. 'One got some sort of infection—horrid it was, and the old lord wouldn't let me get the veterinary—and then there was an old girl who just lay down and wouldn't get up. After two days I felt so sorry for her.'

'You've had no help at all?'

'He was very stubborn, the old lord. When my husband died he said it was no use spending money on the estate when it was just to be owned by...' She hesitated.

'By what?' Finn asked, still gentle.

'*Tuathánach*,' she muttered. 'I'm sorry but that's how he saw you. Which gun?'

'No gun,' Finn said grimly. 'We may be *tuathánach* but sometimes that's a good thing. Put the

guns away, Mrs O'Reilly, and remind us to increase what we're giving you. You've been a hero
but, *tuathánach* or not, we're in charge now. Jo,
get yourself inside out of the rain. Mrs O'Reilly,
could you fetch me a bucket of hot soapy water,
anything I might be able to use for lubricant and
a couple of old sheets and scissors? I'll see what
I can do.'

'I'm staying,' Jo said and he shrugged.

'As you like, but it won't be pretty.'

'Then isn't it good that pretty's not my style.'

'So what's *tuathánach*?'

Mrs O'Reilly had disappeared, off to replace
gun with soap and water. Finn was gently moving his hands over the little cow's flank, speaking
softly—in Gaelic? Did cows understand Gaelic?
Jo wondered. Or maybe it was cow talk. This man
was so big and so gentle...

Did she have a cow whisperer on her hands?

She didn't go near. When she'd gone near any
of the livestock on the place they'd backed with
alarm, but Finn seemed to be able to move among
them with ease. When he'd approached the little
cow she'd heaved and tried to rise but the effort

had been too much. She'd slumped again but the moment he'd touched her, the moment the soft Gaelic words began, she seemed to have lost fear.

Maybe I would too, Jo thought, and then thought maybe she had. She thought back to Finn walking towards her over the bog, to Finn speaking in his soft Irish brogue, to Finn smiling at her, and she remembered how the terror of her situation had disappeared. She'd still been cold and humiliated and stuck but the moment he'd opened his mouth she'd stopped being afraid.

He was just plain lovely, she decided, wiping rain from her face. She was so wet now she was almost past noticing, or maybe it was that she was only noticing Finn. He was kind and he was funny and he was wise and he was strong—and it didn't hurt that he was so darned good-looking as well.

Did the little cow think he was good-looking?

'*Tuathánach* means peasant,' Finn told her. He'd taken a while to answer her question but she was forced to forgive him. You could forgive a lot of a dripping-wet man with his arm up a cow. 'That's what I am.'

'You're Lord of Glenconaill.'

'Who's just ruined a perfectly good shirt. Is that a lordly thing to do?'

'It's definitely a lordly thing to do,' she declared. 'Can I help?'

'If you must stay then you could rip sheets,' he told her. 'Do you faint at the sight of blood?'

'Excuse me?'

He grinned. 'Sorry. I forgot you're *tuathánach*, too. We peasants come from strong stock. But Jo, this'll get messy, I can't guarantee a happy ending and you must be wet and cold. You might want to go inside and wait.'

'Like a lady. Huh? What's the Irish for bastard?'

'Jo...'

'Tell me.'

'*Bastaird*,' he said reluctantly.

'Well, there you go,' she said, and hauled herself up on the stone fence, close enough to watch but not so close as to worry the little cow and the older cow still hovering close. 'A *tuathánach bastaird*. That's not the class who gets to block out the nasties of the world. You do what you have to do. I'm the support team. I might not be much help but I'm cheering from the sidelines.'

She hesitated and then looked at the little cow

and the terror that was unmistakable in the creature's eyes. 'Do you really think you can help her?'

'If not, I do know how to use a gun,' Finn told her. 'I won't push past my limitations but I'll do my best.'

Jo sat on her fence in the rain and cut sheets into strips, as instructed, on the diagonal to give them more strength. 'I could use ropes but sheets will be cleaner and I don't have time to forage in the stables looking for the right type of rope,' Finn told her. So she sat and cut her sheets with care, as if it was very important that she get each line exactly straight. Mrs O'Reilly had brought an armload of linen. She tested each sheet and decided on the coarsest for strength and then worried that it might be too coarse.

She could go inside and do it but she didn't want to. This was a small job but she was focusing fiercely because it was the only thing she could do and she was desperate to help. She was hardly noticing that it was raining.

'Tell me what's happening,' she asked quietly, and she wouldn't have asked at all but Finn was speaking slow and steady to the little cow, as if to reassure her that he was no stranger but a man who knew his job, who was here to help her.

And it was surely working, Jo decided. The more she listened to his soft, reassuring brogue, the more she decided the calf would slip out to listen.

But of course the calf didn't.

'It's a big calf,' Finn told her, still softly, as if still talking to the little cow, though changing from Gaelic to English. Did cows understand Gaelic better?

Gaelic sounded...sexier.

'I'm thinking she's been got at by a bull that's not her breed.' Finn was lying flat in the mud. She couldn't see what he was doing from the angle where she sat but she could see enough to know it was hard. She could see the cow tense with contractions and she could tell by the way Finn's voice changed that the contractions were squeezing his arm.

'I'm suspecting the older cow's someone's house cow,' he said. 'She'll have got out with her nearly grown calf and wandered the roads. Somehow the younger one's been got at by a bull. I'm betting they'll belong to a hobby farmer, someone who spends weekends down here, doesn't care for the land. Doesn't search for missing stock. These two would have starved if Mrs O'Reilly hadn't agreed to take them. And now we get to pick up the pieces.'

'You love it,' she said slowly, hearing the anger in his voice.

'What, this?'

'No, farming.'

'I do.' He gave a grunt of pain. 'This calf has a big head and the legs are tucked back. I'm trying to haul the hooves forward between contractions but there's so little room.'

'Could I help?'

'You!'

' I have small hands. Plus you don't ride bikes like I do without gaining shoulder muscles. Try me.'

'Jo, you don't want...'

'Try me.'

So then it was Jo, lying in the mud, following Finn's directions.

'You need to wait until the contraction backs off to try and bring the hooves forward. But you're doing two things,' he told her. 'While the contraction hits, you need to hold the head back. Feel before the contraction hits, work out how you can cup the skull and push back. As soon as the contraction eases then try and hook the hooves forward. It's tight, and you only have until the next contraction. My hands just won't do it.'

'I'll try.'

'Of course you will,' he said. *'A mhuirnín.* I'm starting to think you can do anything.'

And what was there in that to make her feel warm despite any amount of mud? And determined to do this.

She concentrated. She held the head and rode out a contraction and then manoeuvred her fingers until she felt what she was sure was a leg. Or almost sure. She got a grip and tugged, and the leg slid forward. The hoof was suddenly in front of the little nose.

'I did it,' she breathed but then the next concentration hit and she went back to holding the head because she could still only feel one hoof in front. And the contraction hurt!

But Finn was holding her shoulders and it was okay.

It was okay as long as Finn was holding her.

'You're amazing,' Finn told her and because he said it she decided she was. 'You can do it,' he said and she took a deep breath and tackled the other side. And when the hoof slid up and she had two hooves facing forward she felt as if she were flying.

'I think we're ready,' she said unsteadily.

'Both hooves forward?'

'Yes.'

Finn lubricated his arm and she backed off. He checked, and his face broke into a grin that made her heart twist and the pain in her bruised arm fade to nothing.

'Now it's time for your sheets,' he said and she had to forget about his smile and hand him her strips of sheets and watch as he fashioned ties around the little hooves. Then she watched and waited as he pulled back at every contraction.

She watched as finally the little calf slipped out into the world, as Finn's face broke into the widest grin she'd ever seen.

She had to wait as he cleared the calf's nose and mouth. As he checked her and found her flawless. As he lifted her and carried her round so her exhausted mother could see her, smell her and then tentatively start the first lick of cleaning, of caring, of starting to be...family.

And then she had to hold her breath as Finn turned back to her. For a moment she thought he was getting on with the job of cleaning up.

Instead of which, he drew her gently to him.

And he kissed her.

'Jo Conaill, you are awesome.'

'So are you, Finn Conaill.'

'Yes, we are,' he said and kissed her again. 'You want a shower? It's stopped raining.'

So it had. She hadn't noticed.

Did she want a shower? She drew back and looked down at herself and laughed.

'Maybe.'

'Together?'

And that took her breath away.

She did, she thought. Of course she did. She could let herself sink into this man, into his body, into his smile, into his life.

She wanted to.

But at her feet the little cow mooed softly and struggled to shift so she could lick her calf more effectively and somehow a sliver of sense was gleaned from the pair of them.

Actions had consequences.

She was a loner for a reason.

'I think...separate showers,' she managed, and he hesitated and then nodded.

'That's probably wise.'

It was, but she was having a whole lot of trouble staying wise.

They had a very late lunch, interrupted by constant visits to the window to check how mother and baby were doing. The sun had come out again and they were looking fine.

Even Mrs O'Reilly detoured past the window every time she brought anything to and from the dining room, and she seemed to find a lot of excuses to come to and from the dining room.

'Eh, you've done well, the pair of you,' she said as she served them coffee. She beamed at them as if she was their grandma and all their useful attributes were due to inheritance from her side of the family. Then she whisked herself off and closed the door behind her.

'We did,' Jo said, suddenly just a little self-conscious. Actually, she always was self-conscious in this room. Mrs O'Reilly loved serving them here. She wouldn't hear of them eating in the kitchen but it was so ostentatious. If she had to stay here longer she'd insist on eating somewhere else, she thought. *Tuathánachs* should eat in the kitchen.

Tuathánach bastairds probably ate on the back step.

Which reminded her...

'*A mhuirnín*,' she said out loud and Finn stared.

'Sorry?'

'That's what you called me. What does it mean?'

He coloured, just a bit, which she liked. She liked it when he was disconcerted.

'My sweetheart,' he mumbled. 'Figure of speech.'

'I guess it's better than *tuathánach bastaird*.'

'I guess.' He was blushing, Jo thought with delight. Blushing! But, she reminded herself, she had refused the shower. She needed to get things back on an even keel.

'What will you do with them?' she asked, but he was still distracted.

'Who?'

'The cows.'

'I guess that's for both of us to decide.'

'I can't decide the fate of cows.'

'They won't sell. They're a motley collection of breeds. The calf's a heifer but she's a weird wee thing and they're all scrawny.'

'They could stay here until the farm sells.'

'I guess. I doubt Mrs O'Reilly will want the responsibility. We need to find an overseer until transition.'

'Because we're leaving,' she said flatly and he nodded.

'Because we're leaving.'

Silence.

What was happening? Jo thought. Things should be straightforward. This was an amazing inheritance. They'd sorted almost everything that had to be sorted. Tomorrow the lawyer would come, the papers would be signed and they'd be on their way, an enormous amount richer.

The doorbell pealed and they both started, then looked at each other and grinned. Two identical smiles.

'Are we expecting anyone—dear?' Finn asked, and Jo chuckled. They were sitting at an absurdly formal dining table, sipping coffee from heirloom china, waiting for their housekeeper to open the doors and announce whoever it was. It really was ridiculous.

'I can't think,' she murmured. 'But if it's a gentleman…dear…you'll need to take him into the study for port. The lady needs to retire to her needlework.'

His chuckle matched hers, but he rose and opened the dining room doors, to find Mrs O'Reilly welcoming a rotund little man, bald, beaming and sporting a clerical collar.

'Lord Conaill, this is Father…'

'Adrian,' the little man said, beaming and holding out his hand in welcome. 'No need to stand on ceremony, My Lord.'

'Then it's Finn,' Finn said, taking his hand. Jo watched as the little man pumped Finn's hand with pleasure and then beamed through to her.

'And this must be the castle's new lady. Fiona's daughter. You look like your mother, girl.'

'I'm Jo,' she said shortly.

'Lovely,' the priest said. 'Now, I know you're busy. So much to sort out. So sad about your… grandfather? I've let you be until now, knowing you need time to settle, but I thought I'd pop in now and let you know the whole village is eager to meet you. And when you're ready to join the community...' His beam faded a little. 'Well, your presence will be keenly felt. There's so much need. You know you're the biggest landholder here, and half the village pays you rent. But the land's bad. If you can possibly see your way to do something about the drainage...'

Whoa, Jo thought, but Finn was before her.

'The castle's for sale,' he said and the little man's face dropped.

'Really?'

'Really.'

And he slumped. The life seemed to drain out of him. He closed his eyes for a moment, then took a deep breath and tried to regroup. When he opened his eyes again, his shoulders went back as if bracing and he managed a weak smile to both of them.

'Well,' he said, 'I've heard rumours of the way the old lord treated you both so maybe I'm not surprised, but it's such a shame. I imagine the castle will be bought by foreigners. They almost all are, our stately homes. Corporates, mostly, where company executives can bring colleagues and clients for an Irish jaunt. They do the castles up, but the countryside...' He sighed. 'Well, if you're sure... It's no business of mine to be making you change your mind.'

Silence. Then...

'What's the story on the empty cottages on the road in?' Jo asked, and she said it even before she knew she was going to ask. Why was she asking? Mrs O'Reilly should usher the priest out, she thought, and then she and Finn should get on with sorting the last few things that needed to be done before the lawyer arrived tomorrow.

'The cottages...' the priest repeated and Mrs O'Reilly suddenly sprang to life, like a hunting spaniel at first sight of duck.

'I've just made coffee, Father,' she said. 'Would you be liking some?'

'Well, I would,' the priest told her, and Finn glanced at Jo, startled, and she shrugged because she didn't regret asking. Not really. She was walking away from this place. Surely she should understand what she was walking away from?

Once ensconced in a dining chair, in the midst of the absurd formality of the room, the priest seemed to relax. He took his time with his first couple of sips of coffee, seeming to consider what was best to say and then started. 'There used to be a village much closer to the castle,' he told them. 'That was before the clearing, though.'

'The clearing?' Jo asked, carefully not looking at Finn. She still wasn't sure why she was doing this.

'Nineteenth century,' the priest told her. 'The landlords found they could make a much greater profit if the land was rolled into one holding. The tenants were cleared, and of course the potato famine hit. These cottages seem to stand for ever, though. No lord's ever thought of pulling them down. There was a church here too, though that was pulled down to be used for the making of the church in Killblan. And a school, though that's rubble. I've often thought it would be grand to restore them, put in tenants, like an artists' community or somesuch. Something that could bring life to the district. Something...'

He searched for the right word and finally found it. 'Something fun,' he said at last. 'There's been little fun for a long, long time. No disrespect, but the old lord was a terrible landlord, as was his father and his father before him. I was so hoping...'

But then he stopped. He pushed back his cup

as if he'd just realised he was speaking his own dream. The dream had already been dashed. He closed his eyes and then opened them and gave a brisk nod. Moving on to what was possible.

'But it's naught to do with you,' he said, gently now. 'You'll have your own lives to lead, and what's happening here is our business. I'm sorry to have bothered you. I'll let you get on. Bless you both, the pair of you, with what you decide to do with the proceeds of this place, though I'd be remiss if I didn't say a donation to the building fund of our church in Killblan would be very welcome. But if that's as far as you can manage...' He dredged a smile. 'Well, we're thankful for what we can get.'

And he was gone, with a warm word for Mrs O'Reilly, and not a backward glance at the pair of them. And Finn and Jo were left sitting at the dining table feeling...

Rotten, Jo thought. Really rotten.

Which was unfair. This had nothing to do with her. The family in this castle had rejected her out of hand. She'd been unwanted. The paintings, the tapestries on the walls, had no place for an illegitimate child of the daughter of the house. Neither had they a place for a man who was the descendant of an unwanted 'spare to an heir'.

But...

'What would you do if you stayed?' Finn asked.

CHAPTER EIGHT

WHAT WOULD YOU do if you stayed?

The question didn't make sense. Jo stared at Finn across the table and thought…actually the words did make sense. It was only everything else that didn't.

'What do you mean?' she managed.

'Just what I said.' But he wasn't looking at her. He was staring into the dregs of his coffee cup. 'Just for a moment, just for…fun. As the priest said. Think out of the box. If the lawyer wasn't coming tomorrow, what would you do?'

There was only one answer to that. 'I'd start a tapestry of you with the cows,' she flashed. 'You should be on these walls.'

He smiled, but his smile was strained. 'It'd need to be a portrait of both of us. You with your arm elbow-deep in cow. You could have a caption underneath: "I may need to clean my watch".'

'I'm right, though,' she muttered. 'You should be on the walls.'

'As should you. It's only an accident of birth that we're not. But we don't have a place here, Jo. It's not ours.'

'No.'

'But if it was...'

'What would *you* do?' she asked curiously, and was surprised by the look of passion that flooded his face.

'Drains,' he said. 'As Father Adrian said. I'd see to the drainage here on the castle land but, as he said, on the tenants' land as well. I haven't had time to even look at the tenanted farms but the land's a mess that could be fixed. If I had my way...' And then he stopped and the room was filled with silence.

'What would you do with the cows?' she asked at last.

'The cows?'

'There are three generations of cow looking in the window at us right now.' It wasn't true. They were half a field away but in her imagination Jo had them staring straight at them, knowing their fate was in their hands.

'The sensible thing...'

'You said we're not talking sensible,' she retorted. 'We're talking fun. What would you do... for fun?'

'Keep them to keep the grass down?' He grinned. 'No, okay, the sheep could do that. But we have a newly calved cow who'll produce more milk than her calf needs. It'd be fun to milk her once a day, to have fresh milk whenever we need it. And to watch the calf grow. Those little cows have had a pretty lean time of it. It'd be good to watch them fatten up.'

'But not for the knackery.'

'As you said, I'm talking fun, not sense.' He stared out of the window, across the fields. In the distance were the ruins of the old village settlement the priest had been talking of. 'You know...'

'They'd be great with people in them,' Jo finished for him because that was what she was thinking and maybe he was too? 'What did the priest say? An artists' colony, or somesuch? Wouldn't that be a fun project to bring people to the district? Maybe this castle could even be part bed and breakfast. An upmarket one. Maybe we could cash in on tourists wanting local colour.'

'It'd take a serious amount of money.'

'There is a serious amount of money,' she whispered. 'And we wouldn't have to do it all at once.'

They were staring at each other over the table. Jo could almost see their thoughts bouncing back and forth. There were things she was thinking that she didn't need to say—she could see the reflection of them in his eyes.

'We couldn't,' she said at last, but the frisson of thought kept flashing.

'Why not?' It was taking a while between sentences. They needed space between truly enormous thoughts.

'Your farm...'

'I could sell my farm if I had this one. It'd be a shift in loyalties but I could do it. But you... Jo, we couldn't do this apart. The castle needs the fortune that goes with it. It'd have to be a partnership. You'd have to stay here. You'd have to...settle.'

And there it was, out in all its enormity. Jo was gazing at Finn and he was gazing back. His look wasn't challenging, though. It was...

No. She didn't know what it was, but she did know that there was understanding behind his gaze. As if he knew how torn this whole thing could make her.

If they stopped talking of this as a fantasy... If they decided to make it real...

'You know,' he said thoughtfully when the silence seemed as if it might extend into the middle of next week—when the enormity of what was between them was starting to seem overwhelming— 'we don't need to decide right now.'

'What...what do you mean? The lawyer's coming tomorrow.'

'But I'm the Lord of Glenconaill,' he told her and his grin suddenly flashed out again. 'I'm a man with two suits of armour—okay, one if we share, but maybe one's enough. I believe the Lord of Castle Glenconaill, with or without armour, can decree when and if a lowly Dublin lawyer can and can't visit this castle.'

And Jo thought back to the smooth-speaking, supercilious Dublin lawyer who'd treated them both as if he knew what was best for them and she couldn't help it. She giggled.

'Would you phone him and say, "This is Lord Conaill speaking"?'

'I could do that.'

'Grandpa has a brocade dressing jacket in his room. One of those would be just the thing for such a phone call.'

'And I could say, "Myself and Lady Jo—" for if the priest is referring to you as the lady of the castle, who am I to argue and we're sharing, right? "—Our High and Mightinesses have mutually decided we wish for more time to decide on the fate of our heritage. So please delay your travel…"'

'"My good man",' Jo finished for him and giggled again and then she stopped giggling because what was happening was far bigger than a delay in a lawyer's visit.

Suddenly what was between them was huge.

'We've kissed,' she said, because the kisses were with her still, the way he'd touched her, the way her body had responded. 'It didn't…it doesn't…'

'It might,' Finn told her. He smiled across the table and his smile was enough to make her gasp. His smile was a caress all by itself. 'I guess this would give us a chance to see.'

And that took her breath away. *A chance to see…*

She didn't get attached. She couldn't get attached. She didn't have a home and she didn't want one.

So how had she ended up here, with a castle and a tattered teddy bear and three cows and... Finn?

The concept was terrifying. The concept was exhilarating.

'One day at a time,' Finn said very gently, and she thought, *He does understand. He won't be rushing me.*

But she almost wished he was. She almost wanted him to round the table and take her in his arms and say, *This is where you belong. You're staying here for ever. With me.*

Only that was the siren song. They were the words she'd been waiting a lifetime to hear, only when she had heard them they'd always turned into a lie.

'You want me to make the call?' Finn asked and she tried to think logically but his gentleness shook her logic.

His gentleness that made her want to stay.

'Only if you can do it without the dressing jacket,' she managed. 'Only if you can do it as you.'

'Then it should be a three-way call,' he told her.

'If I'm not doing it as the autocratic Lord of Glenconaill then it should be from you and me, from Finn and Jo, telling him we've decided to stay.'

'But only...'

'Only for a while,' he said, still gently. 'Only until we...see what might happen.'

'You wouldn't sell your farm straight away?'

'I have a manager and staff,' he told her. 'No one else needs me.'

Except someone did.

The call to his manager was tricky.

'I won't be home for a while,' he told Rob and there was a lengthy silence on the end of the phone while Rob thought about it. His manager was a friend of long-standing, and a man of few words. He wasn't a man to rush things. Maybe he'd buy the farm, Finn thought. He could make it easy for him. But that was for the future. Meanwhile...

'What about your Maeve?' Rob asked. 'Her father was here today.'

'Martin came? Did Maeve come with him?'

'She's back in Dublin. People are saying it's over between you, but her father talks like he's still expecting a wedding.'

'It is over,' he said heavily. 'But it's up to Maeve to tell him. I don't know why she won't.'

'Finn...'

'What would you have me do?' he demanded. 'Walk into Martin's living room and say, "I'm not marrying your daughter"? Maeve came over the day I left and asked me to give it a bit more time before she tells him. To be honest, I no longer know what Maeve wants, but it needs to be settled. It was only just okay to pretend before I met...'

And then there was silence.

'Before you met...?' Rob said at last and Finn tried to think of something to say and couldn't.

'This Jo,' Rob ventured. 'The woman you've inherited with. Your cousin?'

'We share the same great-great-grandfather. That's hardly a bar...'

'To what?' Finn could almost see his manager's eyebrows disappearing into his receding hairline. 'Marriage? Whoa.'

'Whoa's right. I hardly know her.'

'You've been in the same castle for a week.'

'It's a very big castle.'

'I'm sure it is.' And his manager was laughing.

'You seem to have yourself in the midst of a love triangle.'

Where was respect when you needed it? he thought. This was what happened when you employed friends. Surely the Lord of Glenconaill should be immune from ribbing. 'That's not the way it is,' he said bluntly. But he thought of Maeve, laying claim to him even now. And he thought of Jo, not laying claim to a thing.

Jo would never claim. She didn't think she had the right.

'There's nothing like that in it,' he said sharply. 'But Rob, the sheep here…I've not seen anything like the quality of their coats. Someone's put a huge amount into their breeding. I'll get you up to see them. I'd like your advice.'

'About breeding?' And Rob was still laughing. 'Of course,' he told him. 'Well, well. We live in interesting times but I think I need to avoid Maeve's father, don't you?'

'Raye?'

It was the first call Jo had made to Australia since she'd arrived; the only call she had to make.

Raye was part owner of the last café she'd worked at. She had Jo's bike in the back of her shed.

'Jo!' Raye was brisk and practical and she sounded rushed. 'Good to hear from you, girl. When can we expect you back?'

'I've been delayed,' Jo told her. 'I'm sorry but I'm not sure when I'm arriving.'

'You know Caroline's heading back to the States next week. She's your fill-in, honey. If you're not back by then I'll have to employ someone else.'

'I know.'

'It's a pity. You're good. But it can't be helped,' Raye said. 'And I can't keep the bike much longer. My son and his mate are driving down from Brisbane next week. I told them they could use the shed for their car. What do you want me to do with it?'

'I'll find a storage place on the Internet and have them pick it up.'

'That'll cost you.'

'Yeah.' She said it flatly. It wasn't Raye's business what she did. It was no one's business but her own.

'It'll have to be collected between eight and ten, one morning before the kids arrive next week,'

Raye said, moving on. 'That's the only time I'm here to hand over the keys. Let me know when.'

'I'll do that.'

'Right then. See you later,' Raye told her and disconnected and Jo stood still and thought Raye had been her boss for six months and hadn't asked why she was staying longer in Ireland or whether she was having a good time or…anything.

She had no personal connection.

That was what she wanted, Jo thought. Wasn't it? It was the background she'd carefully culti-vated since the last disastrous foster home.

But still…

She was sitting on the bed in her Spartan little bedroom. The bald little teddy was sitting beside her. She picked him up and stared down into his lopsided eyes.

'I do like being alone,' she whispered, but she still held him and then Finn's voice shouted along the corridor.

'Jo, I'm heading out to check our calf before bedtime. You want to come?'

'Yes,' she called and then she smiled down at her scruffy, moth-eaten teddy. 'Yes, I do.'

* * *

The calf was fine.

The storm was well past and the night was warm and still, so Finn had decreed the threesome were best left in the field rather than ushered into the sheds. The little cow was placidly nosing her calf while her udder was being prodded and tugged, and the older cow was standing benignly beside them in the moonlight, to all appearances like a doting grandma.

'We've done well,' Finn said. They didn't go close, just stood back and watched. 'A couple of bruised arms for us and a happy ending all round.'

'It is a happy ending,' Jo said softly and then Finn caught her hand in his and held. Strong and warm and fast.

'It could be,' he said and there was all the meaning in the world in those three words.

She didn't pull away. She couldn't, even if she wanted to—which she didn't.

'It's too soon,' she murmured.

'Much too soon,' he agreed. 'But we're giving ourselves time. How long does it take to make the tapestry you're talking of?'

'Months.'

'There you go, then.' He sounded smug.

'Once I draw it I can finish it back in Australia.'

'I can't draft sheep anywhere but here.'

'You could always put in a farm manager and travel back and forth from your home to supervise.'

'So I could,' he said easily. 'If that's what I wanted.'

'Finn...'

'Mmm.'

'It is too fast.'

'It is and all,' he said and then he didn't say anything for a while. They simply stood, hand in hand, in the moonlight while thoughts, feelings, sensations zinged back and forth between them. Things changed. Things grew.

'I should...go to bed,' Jo said at last and the zinging increased a little.

A lot.

'So should I,' Finn told her. 'Noddy's waiting.'

'Your giraffe?'

'And your teddy's waiting for you,' he told her placidly, and she could hear the smile in his voice, even if she couldn't see it in the dark. 'So you'll be sleeping in your tiny bed with your teddy, and

I'll be sleeping in my grand bed with my giraffe. Jo...'

'Mmm?' She was almost afraid to breathe.

'My bed's big enough for four.'

'It's...too soon.'

'Of course it is.' He was instantly contrite. 'Sorry I ever mentioned it. It's just that I thought Noddy and Loppy might sleep better with company.' His hand still held hers, and it felt...okay. 'Same with us,' he told her. 'I'm sure this castle has its share of ghosts. *Taibhse*. I thought I heard them last night, clanking round in the basements. I'm sure I'd sleep better with company.'

'Just to keep the *taibhse* at bay.'

'That's it,' he said cheerfully. 'I'm a 'fraidy cat.'

'I'm very sure you're not.'

'And you, Jo Conaill?' And suddenly his voice lost all trace of laughter. He turned and took her other hand so he had them both and he was gazing down at her in the moonlight. His grip was strong and sure, and yet she knew if she pulled back he'd let her go in an instant. 'Are you afraid, my Jo?'

'I'm not...your Jo.'

'You're not,' he told her. 'As you say, it's too soon. Too fast. Too...scary?'

And yet it wasn't. What was scary about leaving her hands between his? What was scary about taking this giant step into the unknown?

A step towards loving?

Why not? Why on earth not?

'I...it'd be only for Loppy and Noddy,' she ventured, and his smile played out again but it was a different smile, a smile full of tenderness, of promise. Of wonder.

'Only for the children,' he agreed. 'Jo...'

'Mmm?' She could hardly make her voice work.

'Will you let me carry you to our bedroom?'

Our bedroom. There it was, just like that. *Ours.* She'd never had an *ours.*

And to be carried as she'd been carried before, heartbroken, kicking and screaming, being carried away...

But this time she'd not be carried away, she thought. She'd be carried to a bed with Loppy and Noddy. And Finn.

He was waiting for her answer. He'd wait, she thought, this big, gentle man who was the Lord of Glenconaill and yet he wasn't. This man who was just... Finn.

Finn, the man who was holding her hands and

smiling down at her and waiting for her to find the courage to step forward.

Only she didn't need to step forward. He was waiting to carry her. If she could just find the breath to speak.

'Yes, please,' she managed and his grip on her hands tightened. He knew how big this was for her. He knew her fear.

She felt exposed to him, she thought, in a way she'd never let herself be exposed before. This man held her heart in his hands. She'd laid herself open.

She trusted.

'You're sure, *a mhuirnín*?'

'Are you sure that means *my sweetheart*?'

'My sweetheart. My darling. My love. Take your pick.'

'I think,' she said, and her voice was so trembly she had trouble making it work at all, 'that I choose them all.'

And then there was no need for words for Finn's grip on her tightened. Before she knew what he was about he'd swung her up into his arms.

And she didn't fight him. Why would she? There was no need for fighting.

As three little cows basked peacefully under the moonlight, the Lord of Glenconaill carried his lady back into his castle, up the grand staircase and into his bed.

Into his heart.

CHAPTER NINE

THIS WAS A secret world. This couldn't possibly be real—and yet it was.

She was the Lady of the Castle. Castle Glenconaill was hers to wander at leisure, explore, to think about what could be done with all these treasures.

A week ago she'd been going from room to room deciding what was to be kept for some vague family archive—some family that wasn't hers.

Now she and Finn were hauling off dust covers, bouncing on sofas, saying, 'Let's keep this one... no, this one...how about both? How about all?'

She was a kid in a sweet shop, suddenly knowing every sweet could be hers. This world could belong to her and to Finn, and as the days went on it felt more and more wonderful.

It felt right.

Castle or not, it felt like home.

And it had nothing at all to do with the fact that

this was a castle, part of an inheritance so large she could hardly take it in. It had everything to do with the way Finn smiled at her, laughed with her, teased her. With the way Finn took her to his bed and enfolded her body with a passion that brought tears to her eyes.

With the way Finn loved her...

And there was the heart of what was happening. Finn loved her.

It's hormones, she told herself in the moments when she was trying to be sensible. She'd read somewhere that no one should ever make a long-term relationship decision in the first few months of hormonal rush, and yet the decision seemed almost to have been made.

For Finn loved her and she was sure of it. In the closeness of the night he held her and he whispered words to her, sometimes in Gaelic, sometimes in words she knew, but, either way, the meaning was as obvious as the way he held her.

She was loved.

She was...home.

And surely that was the most seductive word of all. Jo Conaill had finally found a place she trusted, a place where she couldn't be turned out on the whim of her ditzy mother or the problems of a troubled foster parenting system. This was a place that was hers. Or, okay, it was half hers but it didn't matter that it was half hers because the other half was Finn's and Finn loved her.

And she loved him.

She loved everything about him. She loved that he was his own man. She loved that even on that first morning, after a night of lovemaking that made her feel as if her world had been transformed entirely, he'd pushed back the covers and smiled down at her and left.

'I need to check the cows.' He'd kissed her and went to check on the newborn calf, and she'd looked out of the window and seen him turn from the cows and gaze out over the land to the sheep grazing in the distance. She knew he cared about so much more than just her.

But then he'd come back to her and they'd showered together and made love again. Afterwards she'd taken more tapestries down to the stream. Life had started again, only rebooted with a different power source.

Rebooted with love and with trust.

It was almost dark now. She was sitting by the

fire sorting threads she'd bought by mail from Dublin. She had enough to start her tapestry.

She could stay here until she finished it, she thought dreamily. She could walk the hills with Finn during the day. She could help him with the stock. They could put off contacting the lawyer until…until…

She didn't want to know until when. She just wanted to *be*.

'Hey.' He'd entered silently. She looked up and smiled, at her Lord of Castle Glenconaill in his stockinged feet, his worn trousers, his sleeves rolled to reveal his brawny arms. Her man of the land. Her lord and her lover.

'Sewing a fine seam, My Lady?'

'Help me sort the threads,' she said calmly. 'I want the blues sorted left to right, pale to dark.'

'Yes, ma'am,' he said and sat and sorted and she sat by the massive fireplace and thought she'd never been so at peace. She could never be any happier than she was right at this moment.

And then, when the blues were in a neat line, he looked up at her and his eyes gleamed in the firelight.

'Threads sorted, My Lady,' he told her. 'The

work of the world is done. The castle's at peace and it's time for the lord of the castle to take his lady to bed. Are you up for it?'

And she grinned like an idiot, smiling into his laughing eyes, falling deeper and deeper.

And when he lifted her into his arms, as he did most nights now, there was no panic.

She was home.

Only of course she wasn't.

Paradise was for fools. How many times had she learned that as a child? Trust was what happened just before the end.

Finn was out with the sheep when he came. It was mid-morning. Jo had taken the farm truck into town to pick up feed supplement for the cows. They'd thought to go together but one of the sheep had caught itself on a fence and lacerated its hind quarters.

'I'm not good with blood,' Jo had said, looking at the sheep with dismay. 'I managed with the calf but that was because I could do it by feel, with my eyes closed. Yikes. Will you need to put it down?'

'I can stitch it.'

'You!'

'There's no end to my talents,' he'd told her, grinning. 'I wasn't always Lord Conaill, able to ring whoever and say, "Stitch it, my good man". Needs must.'

'Can you stop it hurting?' she said dubiously and he'd shown her the kit he always carried in the back of his truck and she'd shuddered and headed for the village so she didn't have to watch.

The sheep wasn't as badly injured as the amount of blood suggested. Finn cleaned, stitched, loaded her with antibiotic and set her free, then stood for a while looking out over the land, thinking of everything he could do with this place. Thinking of everything he and Jo could do with this place.

The prospect almost made him dizzy. This farm and Jo.

He'd never met anyone like her. His loyalties had somehow done a quantum shift. His castle, his lady. Jo made him feel...

'My Lord?' It was Mrs O'Reilly, calling from the top of the ha-ha. She refused to call him anything other than *My Lord* and lately she'd even started calling Jo *My Lady*. Much to Jo's discomfort.

He turned and saw the housekeeper and then he saw who was beside her.

Martin Bourke.

Maeve's father.

Mrs O'Reilly waved and Martin negotiated the ha-ha and came across the field towards him, a stocky, steady man, grizzled from sixty years of farm life, a man whose horizons were totally set on his farm and his daughter.

Finn's heart sank as he saw him. Now what?

'Martin,' he said, forcing his greeting to be easy-going. He held out his hand. 'Good to see you.'

'It's not good to see you,' Martin snapped and stood six feet back from him and glared. 'You're sitting pretty here all right. Lord of Glenconaill. Think you're better than us, do you?'

'You know me better than that, Martin.' He should. Martin Bourke had been his neighbour all his life. Finn and Maeve were the same age. They'd started school together, had been firm friends, had been in and out of each other's houses since childhood.

Maeve had been a friend and then, somehow, a girlfriend. There'd always been an assumption that they were destined to be a pair. But then things had changed...

'You'll come home and marry her,' Martin snapped and Finn thought, *Whoa, that's pushing things to a new level.*

'Martin...'

'I couldn't get any sense out of her. Nothing. That day you left... She came home weeping and went straight back to Dublin and have I got a word of sense out of her since? I have not. I thought there's been a tiff, nothing more, that it was more of this nonsense of giving her space, but yesterday I'd had enough. So I went to Dublin and I walked into this fine bookshop she's been working in and she was standing side on to the door. And I saw... She's pregnant. Pregnant and never a word to me. Her father. Did you know? Did you?'

'I knew,' he said heavily. 'She told me the morning I left.'

'So...'

'Martin, it's not...'

'Don't tell me,' he snapped. 'She says it's nothing to do with you and she'll come home at the weekend and we'll talk about it. Nothing to do with you? When she's been loving you for years?

I know she's got cold feet. Women do, but if a child's on the way it's time to forget that nonsense. Look at you in your grand castle with your grand title. If you think you can walk away from your responsibilities... You'll come home and marry her or I'll bring her here, even if I have to pick her up and carry her. You'll make an honest woman of her, Finn Conaill, or I'll...I'll...'

'You'll what?' Finn said quite mildly. 'Martin, Maeve loves you. That's the only reason she'd marry me—to make you happy. I know that now. Will you push her into marrying a man she doesn't love because she loves you?'

The man stared at him in baffled fury. 'She wants to marry you. The farms... She wants that as much as I do.'

But she didn't. It was the curse of loving, Finn thought. Maeve's mother had died giving birth to the much wanted son who'd been stillborn, and Maeve had been trying to make it up to her father ever since. Until she'd fled to Dublin she'd never had the courage to stand up for what she wanted.

'I'm guessing this woman you have here is the reason,' Martin snapped. 'I saw her in the village when I asked for directions. "Where's the castle?"

I asked, and they pointed to this trollop with pierc-ings and hair cut like a boy and said she's the lady of the castle and would I be looking for her or for her man? And by her man they meant you. And your housekeeper says she's living here. Is that why Maeve's crying her eyes out? If you think you can leave her with a child...'

Finn raked his hair and tried to sort it in his head. He thought of all the things he could say to this man. He thought of all the things he should say.

He could say nothing. It had to come from Maeve. She'd been his friend for ever. She was in trouble and he wasn't about to cut her loose.

'I'll go and see her,' he told him.

'You'll come with me to Dublin. Now.'

'No,' Finn snapped. 'What's between Maeve and me is between Maeve and me. You point a shotgun at the pair of us and it'll make no differ-ence. Leave it, Martin. Go home.'

'You'll leave this trollop and fetch Maeve home?'

'If you ever refer to Jo as a trollop again you'll find your teeth somewhere around your ankles,' he said quite mildly. 'Go home and wait for Maeve.'

Martin left. Finn went inside and cleaned up and thought of what he should do.

Wait until tomorrow? Tell Jo what was happening? But it sounded sordid, he thought. *Jo, I'm going to Dublin to tell my ex-girlfriend to tell her father she's having a baby that's not mine.*

The words made him feel vaguely grubby. And angry. How was he in this mess? He should walk from the lot of them.

But his loyalty held him. Martin had helped him when his father died. Without Martin's help, the farm would have gone under.

And Maeve had been his friend for ever.

He could do this, he thought. He'd make a fast trip to Dublin, sort it out, bang their thick heads together if need be and be back late tonight.

Should he leave a note for Jo? How could he? How to explain the unexplainable?

He swore.

And then he lightened. This was the last obligation, he thought. The last link tying him to his old life.

He could do this and then come home to Jo. He could tell her what had happened face to face, and then they could move on with their life together. Here.

This was the start of a new loyalty, to this castle and to each other.

'He's had to go to Dublin on family business. He'll be back late tonight. He said don't worry and he'll explain things when he gets back.'

Jo stared at Mrs O'Reilly in bemusement. She wasn't so much worried about what the housekeeper was saying. There were any number of reasons why Finn could suddenly be called away. After all, he'd left his farm for longer than he'd intended. Things could go wrong. But it was the way the housekeeper was saying it, as if there was a well of titillating facts behind the words.

She wouldn't enquire, she decided. Finn's business was Finn's business.

She headed for the stairs. She needed to wash. One of the bags had split when she'd hauled it out of the truck. She'd scooped it back together but cow food supplement stank.

But Mrs O'Reilly didn't move and then she spoke again.

'He's got another woman and she's in the family way.' The housekeeper's words came out as a gasp. 'I shouldn't say, but girl, it's true. Her father came today, shouting, threatening, mad as fire. Five months gone, she is, and when's he going to marry her? That's what her dadda's demanding! And it seems she's in Dublin, all alone, and your man's saying it's naught to do with him. And I shouldn't have heard but sound carries across the fields and such anger... Two bulls at each other's throats. "You make an honest woman of her", her father said and loud enough to be heard from Dublin itself. So off they went, separate though, His Lordship looking grim as death and her father looking like he wanted his gun. And I don't like to break it to you, when you've been so good to me, but hiding things behind your back... Well, it's best you know. I'm sorry.'

Silence. Jo didn't say a word.

She couldn't.

What was there to say?

He's got another woman and she's in the family way.

This had been a fairy tale, she thought in the tiny part of her brain that wasn't filled with white noise. This inheritance, this castle, this...love story? This fantasy that she could possibly have found her home.

But fairy tales came to an end, and happy ever after... Well, that was just part of the fantasy. What happened to Cinderella after she married her prince? Did he go on being a prince while she went back to sitting by the fireside waiting for the snippets of time he was prepared to give her?

There was so much rushing through her head. Hammering at her were the times as a kid when she'd started feeling secure, feeling loved. *'Would you like to be our child? Would you like this to be your home?'*

She should never, ever have trusted.

'He'll be back for a late dinner,' Mrs O'Reilly said, sounding frightened. 'He said he just needed to sort things at home. He said not to worry. He'll be back before you know he's been gone.'

'You're...sure?' she managed. 'That there's another woman.'

'"My Maeve..."' Mrs O'Reilly told her, and she was quoting verbatim. 'That's what her dadda said. "You've been sweet on each other for ever," he said. "Look at you in your grand castle with your grand title and if you think you can walk away from your responsibilities… You'll come home and marry her or I'll bring her here, even if I have to pick her up and carry her.'"

And there was that word again. Home.

It was such a little word, Jo thought bleakly. It was thrown around by those who had such things as if it didn't even matter.

You'll come home.

He'd said he'd had a long-term girlfriend, she thought dully, but she hadn't asked for details. It wasn't her business. But how could he make love to her, knowing what was in the background?

A woman called Maeve.

A baby.

'I'll make you some lunch,' Mrs O'Reilly said uneasily. 'Things always look better when you're fed.'

Right, Jo thought. *Right?*

She wanted, suddenly, desperately, to go home.

Home?

Home was her bike, she thought. Home was Australia—all of Australia. Home was wherever her wheels took her.

Home was certainly not in some great castle.

Home was not with Finn.

'I need to take some tapestries out of the stream,' she said and was inordinately pleased with the way her voice sounded. 'I'll set them out in the long room—the sun's warm in there. Would you mind turning them for me as they dry? Every couple of hours or so. I dry them flat but they need a wee shake every couple of hours just to get them ventilated underneath.'

'Why can't you do it?' the housekeeper asked, but by the look on her face she already knew.

'Because I don't belong here,' Jo told her. 'Because it's time I went...home.'

It was a long journey to Dublin, a fraught time, and then an even longer journey back to the castle.

Why couldn't they have sorted it between them? Still, at least it was done. Maeve's Steven was a wimp, Finn decided. He was even weaker than Maeve. No wonder they'd feared facing Maeve's father. He should have taken the two of them in hand a month ago and made them face the music. But at least it was now out in the open. Maeve's father was still blustering, but Finn was out of the equation.

'At least now I can organise a wedding,' Maeve

had sobbed and he'd managed a smile. He knew Maeve. Now her father's distress had been faced, pregnant or not, she'd have a dozen bridesmaids and she'd have a glorious time choosing which shade of chiffon they'd all wear.

Jo wouldn't be into chiffon. The thought was a good one and he was smiling as he entered the castle, smiling at the thought of lack of chiffon but smiling mostly because Jo was here and he'd been away all day and she'd smile at him…

Only she wasn't.

'She's left,' Mrs O'Reilly said, and handed him an envelope before stalking off towards the kitchen. She slammed the door behind her so hard the castle seemed to vibrate.

He stood in the entrance hall staring down at the envelope, thinking, *What the…?*

Read it, he told himself but it took a surprising amount of resolution to slit the envelope.

It was brief.

I should have asked about your background. That's my dumb fault. You know all about me and I was so happy I didn't want to know that you had happy families playing in the background. But now Mrs O'Reilly says you have a woman called Maeve and she's five months pregnant. Happy families? I don't know what this is all about but you know what? I don't need to know. All I know is that nothing's solid. Nothing's true. I've known it for ever, so how dumb can I be for forgetting? For hoping things could change?

Finn, I know you want to farm the castle land and, thinking about it, I want you to have it. You're the Lord of Glenconaill and it seems right that your place is here. I know you can't maintain the castle without the fortune, but I don't need a fortune. I mean that, Finn. I'm no martyr, but I have a bike and I make good coffee. I'm free and that's the way I like it.

So I'll write to the lawyer from Australia. I won't be a total doormat—I'd like enough to buy myself a small apartment so if I ever fall off my bike I have security, and I'd like to upgrade my bike, but the rest is yours. It's the way it should be. For you're part of a family, Finn, in a way I never can be. In a way I don't want to be. Being a family is a promise I don't know how to keep.

So that's it. Don't feel guilt over what's hap-

pened. I'm over it already and I'm used to moving on. Keep the cows safe. Oh, and I'll do some research and send you details of someone who can be trusted to restore the tapestries.

Despite all this, I wish you all the best, now and for ever.
Jo

He stood in the entrance hall and stared blindly at the letter.

All the best, now and for ever.
Jo.

For ever.

Then he swore so loudly that Mrs O'Reilly came scuttling back from the kitchen.

'I need to go to Dublin,' he snapped.

'There's no use.'

'What do you mean, no use?'

'I heard her on the phone. She got one of the last tickets on tonight's flight to Sydney. That's why she had to rush.' She glanced at her watch. 'Her plane would be leaving now. Poor girl.'

The door crashed closed again and Finn stood

where he was, letting his emotions jangle until he felt as if his head was imploding. Then he walked out to the field where the little cows stood. The calf was suckling. The light was fading and the mountains in the background were misty blue.

This place was heaven. This place called him as nothing ever had before.

Except Jo.

He should have told her. He should have talked of his problems. Even though what was between him and Maeve was essentially private, essentially over, even, he conceded, essentially humiliating, he should have shared.

He could phone her, he thought. As soon as she reached Sydney...

Did he have a number? No.

Email then? No.

Follow her? Catch the next flight? Pick her up and bring her home?

Home. The word was a sudden jolt, tumbling through his jumbled thoughts. Where was home?

Home could be here, he thought, gazing out at the land of the Conaills, of the land of his forebears. He could make this wonderful. This place should be where his loyalty lay.

But Jo…

Being a family is a promise I don't know how to keep.

How could Jo fit into his vision of home? Into his vision of loyalty?

He couldn't pick her up and carry her anywhere. Did he want to?

He was suddenly thinking back over twenty years, to the night of his father's funeral, sitting in the flower-filled living room trying to stem his mother's inconsolable weeping. He was the oldest and he'd been thought of as the bright one of the family. There'd even been talk of him going to university. But never after that night.

'Please don't leave us,' his mother had sobbed. 'If you leave the farm I'll never be able to support the young ones. Finn, I need you to be loyal to this farm. It's our home.'

So he'd built it up until he could survey it with pride. He'd thought he loved it but now…

He stood in the stillness and wondered whether it was the farm he'd loved or was it the people who lived there? He'd thought of selling it to move to the castle. Love, then, wasn't so deep.

And Maeve? Had he loved Maeve or was it

home and place that she represented? She'd been his friend and that friendship had morphed into something more. But caught up in his relationship was his love for the land and Maeve's loyalty to her father. And overriding everything was her father's unswerving loyalty to his farm.

Maeve's father had encouraged their courtship since they were teenagers, aching for the farms to be joined. He'd almost lost his daughter because of it.

The night wore on. His thoughts were jumbled, confusing jolts of consciousness he was having trouble sorting, but he was getting there.

He was moving on from Maeve...sorting the mess that loyalty to place had caused...

He was focusing on this castle and Jo.

He'd fallen for the two of them. From the time he'd first seen the castle he'd felt a deep, almost primeval urge to work on this land, to restore this estate to what it could be. But part of that urge was the fact that Jo was in the deal. He knew it now because Jo wasn't here and the place felt empty. Desolate.

His thoughts moved back, to Maeve and her father and the not too subtle blackmail.

'If you love me you'll never leave,' Martin had told his daughter. 'This is our farm. Our place. Marry Finn and we'll join the boundaries. It's our home.'

He'd thought this castle could be home. He'd thought this place could hold his loyalty.

He thought of Jo, heading back to Australia. With no home.

Her home should be here.

And then he thought, *Why?* Why should it be here?

What cost loyalty?

He stood and stared at the distant mountains and he felt his world shift and shift again.

Jo.

Home?

CHAPTER TEN

THREE WEEKS LATER saw Jo running a beach café on the south coast of New South Wales.

She hadn't returned to work in Sydney—why would she? She didn't want work colleagues asking how her trip went. Instead she'd ridden south, to a small holiday resort gearing down for the Australian winter. The owners had a new baby, the baby was colicky and when Jo answered the advertisement she was offered as much work as she wanted. She took a vacant room above the shop and got on with her life.

Except she missed things. Things she wasn't allowed to miss?

She worked long hours, from breakfast to dinner. At night she'd pull out her partly done tapestry, of Finn beside cow and calf, with the castle in the background. She wanted it done but she couldn't work on it for long.

It was because she was tired, she told herself,

but she knew it was more than that. She could hardly bear to look at it.

Sleep was elusive and her dreams were always the same.

Now, three weeks after she'd arrived back in Australia, she woke at dawn feeling as if she hadn't slept. But work was calling. Even this early, she knew she'd have locals waiting for the café to open. By now she knew them all and they treated her as a friend.

But she wasn't a friend.

'Don't get too attached,' she muttered to herself as she headed downstairs and saw them waiting through the glass doors. 'I'm itinerant. I should have a sign round my neck that says Born To Move On.'

And then she paused because it wasn't just her usual locals waiting. There was someone behind them. Someone with deep brown hair with hints of copper. A big man, half a head taller than anyone else. A man with green eyes that twinkled in the early morning light. Strikingly good-looking. Gorgeous!

A man called Finn.

Her heart did some sort of crazy backflip and

when it landed it didn't feel as if it was in the right position. She stopped on the stairway, trying to breathe.

She should head back upstairs, grab her things and run. For a dizzy moment she considered the logistics of hurling her bag from the window, shimmying down the drainpipe and leaving.

But Finn had come and her locals were looking up at her in concern.

'Jo?' Eric-the-retired-librarian called through the glass door, no doubt worried that she'd stopped dead on the stairway and wasn't rushing to cook his porridge. 'Are you okay? Should we wake Tom and Susy?'

Tom and Susy were the owners and she'd seen their light on through the night. She knew they'd been up with their baby daughter. She couldn't do that to them.

So no shimmying down drainpipes.

Which meant facing Finn.

'You can do this,' she muttered to herself and somehow she put on a cheery smile and headed down and tugged the doors open.

It was brisk outside, with the wind blowing cold off the ocean. Her locals beetled to their normal tables clustered round the embers of last night's fire. Eric started poking the embers and piling on kindling.

None of them seemed to notice that Finn Conaill had walked in after them.

'Good morning,' he said, grave as a judge, and she almost choked.

'What are you doing here?'

'I'm here for coffee,' he told her. 'And a chat but maybe it should wait until we're fed. Eric tells me you make excellent porridge and great coffee. Could I help you in the kitchen?'

'No!' she said, revolted, and then she looked closer and realised he was wearing leathers. Bike leathers?

He looked...cold.

'Where have you come from?' she managed and he smiled at her then, a tentative smile but it was the smile she remembered. It was the smile that told her her world could never be the same now this man had entered it.

'From Ireland three days ago,' he told her. 'But it's taken me all that time to organise a bike. I wanted the biggest one but hiring one's impossible, so I had to buy. I picked it up from a Sydney dealer last night.'

'You rode from Sydney this morning?'

'I did.' He even looked smug.

'On a bike.'

'Yes.'

'I didn't know you rode.'

'There's lots of things we don't know about each other yet,' he told her and smiled again, and oh, that smile...

He was tugging his gloves off. She reached forward and touched his fingers, a feather-touch, just to see. His fingers were icy.

'Wh...why?' How hard was it to get that one word out? And of course she knew the answer. He wouldn't come from Ireland to Australia without a reason. He'd come to see her.

Maybe this was the Lord of Glenconaill being noble, she thought wildly. Maybe he was objecting to the letter she'd sent to the lawyer. She'd listed what she could use from the estate and she'd stated that the rest was Finn's. He could do what he wanted with it, with or without a woman called Maeve.

'I've come home,' he told her, and the jumble of thoughts came to a jarring halt.

Home?

The word hung. Behind them the locals had abandoned tending the fire. They weren't bothering to peruse the menu they always perused even though they must have known it off by heart for years, but instead they were looking at them with bright curiosity.

They lived here, Jo thought wildly. She didn't. Home was nowhere.

'What do you mean, you've come home?' she demanded and if she sounded snappish she couldn't help it. Of all the stupid things to say...

'It seems a good place,' Finn said, looking around the cosy café with approval. 'Nice fire, or it will be. Warm. Good view. And porridge, I'm told. What's not to like? This'll do us until we move on.'

'Finn!'

'Jo.' He reached forward and took her hands. His really were freezing. She should tug him forward to the fire, she thought. She should...

What she should do was irrelevant. She couldn't

move. She was standing like a deer caught in head-lights, waiting to hear what this man would say.

'I should have told you about Maeve,' he said. 'It was dumb not to tell you. When I first came to the castle, when I first met you, I had a worry about Maeve in the background. In retrospect, I should have shared that worry with you.'

'You should have shared that worry with her,' she managed and it really was a snap now. 'You're having a baby and you don't even talk about it? You don't mention it? Like it's no big deal. That's like my mother...'

'It's not like your mother.' She copped a flash of anger from him then. 'I know your mother thought a baby was no big deal.' The grip on her hands tightened and she could hear his anger in his voice. 'Have a baby, head back to Ireland, re-fuse to sign adoption papers? Your mother used the fate of her child to try and shame her father, and that seems a very big deal to me. I wish she was alive so I could tell her.'

'But you and Maeve...'

'Jo, it's not my baby.' He paused and his anger faded. His voice became gentle. 'Maeve and I have been best of friends since we were five years old.

We always assumed we'd marry. Why not? We loved each other. We always have and we still do. But Maeve's dad is the worst kind of emotional blackmailer. Her mum died when she was seven, and she spent her childhood trying to make him happy. But making her father happy was always a huge ask. He dreamed that we'd marry, that I'd be the son he lost when his wife died in child-birth. We'd join our two farms together, make the empire he'd always dreamed of. It made me un-easy, but I loved Maeve and there was no point in fighting it.'

'You loved Maeve…' She was struggling. They should find somewhere private to talk, she thought. Somewhere like the kitchen. But her onlookers seemed fascinated. Keep the punters happy, she decided, and then she decided she was pretty close to hysteria.

'When you grow up with someone, you do love them,' Finn told her. 'They become…family. I know you don't get that, Jo. I'm hoping I can teach you.'

'But Maeve…'

'Maeve and I loved as best friends,' he told her, smiling down at her with a smile that did her head in. 'And Maeve's father used her loyalty to him and to his farm to coerce her. I never guessed the pressure. More fool me, but then...' He shrugged. 'I was one-eyed about my farm as well so maybe I was part of the problem. Marrying Maeve was just an extension of that loyalty. But over a year ago she found the strength to run. She told her father—and me—that she needed time out before marrying and she took a job in a bookshop in Dublin. And promptly met the owner and fell in love. Really, truly in love. She was so much in love that for the first time in our lives she didn't want to talk to me about it. But her father's emotional blackmail continued. He's had one heart attack and terrified her with the thought of another. She kept telling both of us that she just wanted space.'

'Which broke your heart?' she ventured. She was finding it hard to breathe here. He was so close. He was here. *Finn.*

He grinned at that. 'Um...no,' he conceded. 'Sure, I was puzzled, and yes, my pride was hurt, but we've been apart for over twelve months now. And in truth I wasn't all that upset. Maybe a part of me was even relieved. But then she told me she was pregnant and she wanted me to face her father with her. She thought it might make things better if I was there when she told him, but I thought it'd make things worse. I thought she should face him with Steven, the father of her baby, and I told her so.'

'Oh...' She'd forgotten her audience. She'd forgotten everything. 'Oh, Finn...'

'So that's where it was when I came to the castle,' Finn told her. 'Maeve and I were over. That's when I met you and that's when I knew for certain that Maeve was right. What she and I had was nothing compared to how I felt about you.'

And what was a girl to say about that? Nothing, Jo decided. Nothing seemed to be working. Certainly not her voice. She seemed to be frozen.

'She still didn't have the gumption to face her father,' Finn told her. 'But he finally discovered she was pregnant. Instead of confronting her, he came to find me.'

'And you went...'

'To knock some sense into the three of them,' he told her. 'Yes, Maeve was still terrified but I collected the family doctor on the way back to her father's farm. It was insurance, and her father turned purple with rage and distress, but there wasn't a twinge of heart trouble. They survived and it's sorted. They're about to live happily ever after; that's assuming they have enough gumption to find their way out of a paper bag. But enough of Maeve. Jo, I came here to talk about you. About us. And even about marriage?'

There was a concerted gasp behind them. Jo tried to speak. She couldn't.

And then her locals took over.

'You've come all the way from Ireland to propose?' It was a snap out of left field. Eric had abandoned his fire lighting and now he stalked up to Finn like a small, indignant cockerel. 'So who are you to be asking?' He poked him in the chest. 'You can't just sweep in here and carry her off.'

'Ooh, maybe he can,' one of the ladies behind him twittered. 'He's beautiful.'

'He's a biker. A biker!'

'So's she.'

'Yes, but…'

But she was no longer listening to her locals. She was only listening to Finn.

'Jo, I'm not here to carry you anywhere,' he said softly, smiling at her now, his lovely, gentle smile that kick-started her heart and had it doing handsprings. 'I wasn't so much thinking of me carrying you off but us riding into the sunset together. But there's no rush.' His grip on her hands was infinitely gentle. They were warming, she thought. She was feeding him warmth.

It was a two-way street. The zing between the two of them...

'I'm not here to take you back to the castle,' Finn told her. 'Jo, I'm not here to take you anywhere. I'm here because I'm home.'

'What...?' It was so hard to make her voice work. 'I don't understand.' When her voice finally did work it came out as almost a wail.

'Because where you are is my home,' he said softly and he drew her a little closer so his lips could brush her hair. 'That's what I figured. And I also figured how I'd loved you back in Ireland was dumb. I just assumed you'd be part of the package. Castle and Jo. We'd marry, I hoped, and live in our castle for ever. But then you were gone and I looked around the castle and thought: I don't love the castle. It's just a thing. It's just a place. How can I love a thing or a place when the only way I can truly love is to love you?'

Then, as she said nothing—for how could she think of a single thing to say?—his grip on her hands became more urgent. 'Jo, you said you don't know how to do family. You said you don't do home. But, the way I see it, home is us. Family is us. As long as you and I are together we don't have to strive for anything else. No castles. No farms. Nothing. Not even our bikes if we don't want them.'

Bikes. It was a solid word, the one tangible thing she was able to get her head around. She looked out through the door and saw a great, gleaming Harley parked to the side.

'I don't...I don't have a Harley yet,' she managed which, in the circumstances, made no sense at all.

'We can fix that. We don't have to but we can if we want. Jo, if you'll let me stay we can do anything we want.'

'You want the castle,' Jo whispered.

'Not as much as I want you.'

'Your farm...'

'I'm selling the farm. Where you go, that's where I belong.'

'So you'd follow me round like a stalker...' She

was fighting to keep things light but she was failing. Miserably.

And Finn got serious.

'I wouldn't do that to you, Jo,' he said softly. 'If you say the word I'll go back to Ireland. Or I'll get on my bike and ride around Australia to give you more time to think about it. The decision's yours, love. I won't carry you anywhere and I won't follow unless you want. All I ask is that I love you but that love's dependent on nothing but your own beautiful self. Not on location, loyalty, history. Simply on you.'

'So...' She was starting to feel almost hysterical. How could she believe this? It was a dream. How could she make her thoughts work? 'You'll just abandon the castle? The sheep?'

'That's why it's taken me three weeks to be here. That and the fact that you weren't kind enough to leave a forwarding address. I had to take our slimy lawyer out to dinner and ply him with strong drink before he'd give me your mail address and it took sheer force of personality to make your last employer tell me who'd checked recently on your references. And then I had to find someone to take care of the livestock because I don't like

Mrs O'Reilly's cure by gun method. Luckily she has a nephew who's worked the land with his dad and he seems sensible. So our castle's secure in case we ever wish to come back, but if we decide we don't want to come back then we can put it on the market tomorrow. The world's our oyster. So love... As your astute customer suggested, I'm here to propose, but there's no rush. While you're thinking about it...maybe you could teach me to make porridge?'

'Excellent,' Eric said darkly but he was punched by the lady beside him.

'Eric'll make the porridge,' she said. 'You two go outside and have your talk out. Though can I suggest you head to the side of the shed because the wind's a killer.'

'He can't go down on one knee behind the shed,' Eric retorted. 'It's gravel. And I don't know how to make porridge.'

'That's what the instructions on the packet are for,' the woman retorted. 'And it's only you eating it.' She turned to face Finn. They were all facing Finn. 'So, young man, do you want to pick her up and carry her somewhere you can propose in privacy?'

'I'll carry her nowhere she doesn't wish,' Finn said and his smile was gone and the look he gave Jo was enough to make her gasp. 'Do you wish me to take you outside and propose?'

And there was only one response to that. Jo looked up at Finn and she smiled through unshed tears. She loved this man so much.

He'd given up his castle for her.

He loved her.

'I do,' she whispered and then, because it wasn't loud enough, because it wasn't sure enough, she said it again, three times for luck.

'I do, I do, I do.'

They stayed until the owners' baby had outgrown her colic. They stayed until Jo had not a single doubt.

She woke each morning in the arms of her beloved and she knew that finally, blessedly, she'd found her home.

The two bikes sat outside waiting, but there was little chance—or desire—to use them. Finn refused wages. 'I'm a barista in training,' he told the owners when they demurred. 'Jo's teaching me to make the world's best coffee.' But they worked side by side and they had fun.

Fun was almost a new word in Jo's vocabulary and she liked it more and more.

She loved the way Finn watched her and copied her and then got fancy and tried new ways with the menu and new ways of attracting punters. She loved the way he made the customers laugh. She loved the way he failed dismally to make decent porridge. She loved the way the locals loved him.

She loved him.

And each night she loved him more, and finally she woke and knew that a line had been crossed. That she could never go back. That she truly trusted.

She was ready for home.

'Surely a man's home is his castle,' she told him. 'Let's go.'

'Are you sure?' He was worried. 'Jo, I'm happy to be a nomad with you for the rest of my life.'

'Just as I'm starting to love not being a nomad,' she chuckled and then got serious. 'Finn, I've been thinking... We could do amazing things with our castle. We could run it as an upmarket bed and breakfast. We could ask Mrs O'Reilly to help us if she wants to stay on. We could make the farm fantastic and set up the little cottages for rent by artists. We could work on the tapestries...'

'*We?*'

'If you want.'

'I'm bad with a needle,' he told her. They were lying in bed, sated with loving, and their conversation seemed only partly vocal. What was between them was so deep and so real that it felt as if words hardly needed to be said out loud.

'You're dreadful at porridge too,' she said lovingly. 'What made you try a porridge pancake? Eric'll never get over it.'

'It was a new art form,' he said defensively. 'It stuck on the bottom. I'd made a crust so I thought I'd use it.'

She chuckled and turned in the circle of his arms. 'Finn Conaill, I love you but I've always known you're not a maker of porridge. You're a farmer and a landowner. You're also the Lord of Glenconaill, and it's time the castle had its people. It's time for us to make the castle our home.'

'It's up to you, love. Home's where you are,' he said, holding her close, deeply contented. And she kissed him again and the thing was settled.

They went back to Ireland. They returned to Castle Glenconaill. Lord and Lady ready to claim their rightful place.

And three months later they were married in the village church, with half the district there for a look at this new lord and his lady.

And they decided to do it in style.

In the storeroom were wedding dresses, the most amazing, lavish wedding gowns Jo had ever seen. Soon they'd give them to a museum, they'd decided, but not until they'd had one last use from them.

She chose a gown made by Coco Chanel, worn by her grandmother, a woman she'd never met but whose measurements were almost exactly hers. It was simplicity itself, a wedding gown straight out of the twenties, with a breast-line that clung, tiny slips of silk at the shoulders and layered flares of creamy silk with embroidery that shimmered and sparkled and showed her figure to perfection.

Its nineteen-twenties look seemed as if it was her natural style. With her cropped curls, a dusting of natural make-up and a posy of wild flowers, she was stunning. All the villagers thought so.

So did Finn.

But Jo wasn't the only one who'd dressed up. Finn had dressed up too, but the twenties were a bit too modern, they'd decided, for a true Lord of Glenconaill. 'Breeches,' Jo had decreed and he'd groaned and laughed and given in. They'd chosen a suit that was exactly what Jo imagined her hero should wear. Crisp white shirt and silk necktie. A magnificently tailored evening jacket in rich black that reached mid-thigh. Deep black breeches that moulded to his legs and made Mrs O'Reilly gasp and fan herself.

A top hat.

It should have looked foppish. It should have looked ridiculous. It didn't. Bride and groom stood together as they became man and wife and there was hardly a dry eye in the congregation.

'Don't they look lovely,' their housekeeper whispered to the woman beside her in the pew. 'They're perfect. They're the best Lord and Lady Glenconaill we've ever had.'

'That's not saying much.' The woman she was talking to was dubious. 'There's been some cold souls living in that castle before them. Kicking out younger sons, disowning daughters, treating their staff like dirt.'

'Yeah.' Mrs O'Reilly's nephew was standing beside them, looking uncomfortable in a stiff new suit. He'd spent the last three months working side by side with Finn and if he had his way he'd be there for ever. 'But that's what toffs do and Finn and Jo aren't toffs. They might be lord and lady but they're... I dunno...okay.'

'Okay' in Niall's view was a compliment indeed, Mrs O'Reilly conceded, but really, there were limits to what she thought was okay. And something wasn't.

For the bride and groom, newly married, glowing with love and pride, were at the church gate. Jo was tossing her bouquet and laughing and smiling and they were edging out of the gate and then the rest of the gathering realised what Mrs O'Reilly had realised and there was a collective scandalised gasp.

For they'd grabbed their helmets and headed for Finn's bike, a great beast of a thing, a machine that roared into life and drowned out everything else.

And Jo was hiking up her wedding dress and climbing onto the back of the bike and Finn was climbing on before her.

'Ready?' he yelled back at her, while the crowd backed away and gave them room. Roaring motorbikes did that to people.

'I'm ready,' she told him. 'Ready for the road. Ready for anything. Ready for you.'

And he couldn't resist. He hauled off his helmet and turned and he kissed her. And she kissed him back, long and lovingly, while the crowd roared their approval.

'Ready for the rest of our lives?' Finn asked when finally they could speak.

'Ready.'

'Ready for home?'

'I know I am,' Jo told him and kissed him again. 'Because I'm already there.'

* * * * *